Odd Numbers

JJ MARSH

PREWETT
BIELMANN

Odd Numbers

Cover design: JD Smith

Published by Prewett Bielmann Ltd.

All enquiries to admin@jjmarshauthor.com

First printing, 2020

ISBN 978-3-9525191-5-8

For Janet Davies, Simon Machin, Simon Lee, David Jones and Stephen Whiteman, because it was a big deal

Prologue: Gael, now

Twenty years. In the beginning, grief is a crushing weight you're convinced you cannot bear. After two decades, you can bear it but the effort changes you. The others have altered too, an extra line on the brow, a slight stoop, a shadow behind the eyes. Although no one liked to talk about it. Over the years, our gatherings have become less of a memorial to death and more a celebration of life. Our lives go on. That's the strange thing about this biennial tradition: the more comfort and reassurance it brings, the worse that silent sense of guilt. Five university friends, now spread across the globe, return every twenty-four months for New Year's Eve. We celebrate, but it's also a punishment for the horrible events of 1999. Sometimes I question why we do it to ourselves.

Grief and guilt have combined into an alloy, a chain which over the years stretched a little longer. Sometimes I forgot it was there. But then, just as a walk breaks into a run, the chain pulls tight, tying me like a yard dog to what happened on 31 December twenty years ago. Maybe it's the same for the others, I couldn't say.

Twenty years. Finally, it was my turn to organise one of our reunions. It wasn't deliberate that I always ended up at the back of the queue. Every time it was Gael's year, circumstances changed. Someone had a better idea or an insider tip or an offer we couldn't refuse. But in 2019, the responsibility for the New Year's Eve party was all mine.

My chalet suggestion was an immediate winner. Of course I'd given them other options, though none as attractive as a Swiss chalet in the Alps. It had everything: a big kitchen, enough space for each of us to have privacy, a fireplace and that cosy feeling of being protected from the winter. Just perfect for the twentieth anniversary of our friendship. It should have been our best NYE ever. As it turned out, it was our last.

I sometimes wonder if we would have stayed friends without the shared trauma of loss. If Dhan was still with us, would we have enough reason to meet every two years? In my memory, we were the closest gang of mates, completely inseparable and would have stayed that way forever. But how much of that closeness was created in retrospect? Perhaps the five of us cleaved to each other to close the gap. That gap where number six should be.

Dhanesh. I pictured his face, black eyes flashing with animation, eyebrows as mobile as bats and white teeth inviting me to join in his amusement. His voice with its South London vowels and how he used to ham up an Indian accent for laughs. I closed my eyes with an audible sigh. Twenty years on and I still missed him.

My mind slipped its leash and wandered back to that night twenty years ago. I tried to drag myself back to the present or the future but the path to the past was well worn and familiar. You can't spend twenty years thinking about the same event and just suddenly stop. The mind doesn't work that way. At least, this mind won't.

Chapter 1: Gael, 1999

The country retreat was Dhan's idea. Somewhere out in the back of beyond, away from all the hype and expectation, shitty fireworks and crappy parties. Just us and the natural world as we watched the passing of a millennium. It surprised me to see Mr Life-and-Soul eschew the celebrations of a lifetime, but he insisted the night should be meaningful. He hit every syllable of that word.

We agreed. Of course we did. Where else would we go and who with? The six of us spent every significant moment together. More importantly, we shared the insignificant ones too. We were best friends, a cosy clique and when I look back at those times now, I would describe us as an unhealthy co-dependency. Twenty years ago, I didn't know that expression existed.

When Mika offered his place near Prague and told us about the lake; that was totally unexpected. Simone caused a fuss because that is what Simone does. Jumping into a frozen lake, was he crazy? The lake might be dirty and we would all get sick! What if something went wrong with the sauna? There was no one around for kilometres! Who would rescue us?

When Simone flapped, her voice grew higher and her French accent more pronounced. Her theatrical alarm made it easy to laugh at her, despite the fact she voiced everyone's fears. We each adopted our usual roles. Dhan made jokes, turning one of her silk scarves into a superhero's cape and promising to rescue her. Lovisa sat beside her, holding her hand and addressing her concerns with practical answers. Clark teased her about being a French drama queen and Mika played the paterfamilias. He repeated how his family did this every year and nobody had even so much as suffered a scratch. Dhan did his Flipper routine; arms stiff, body bobbing, wide eyes and huge grin. No one could resist the performing dolphin, even if one was unlikely to be present in a Czech lake.

The imminent adventure sounded like a break from the norm. This was an opportunity to be part of things and I'd be damned if I'd let the girls' side down. Choosing my moment, I announced I was going to jump into the frozen lake and no one could stop me. Lovisa gave me a high-five. Simone's protests subsided into shrugs and sighs. Until she saw the lake.

After our respective Christmas celebrations, we were giddy and overexcited to get away, just as we should be. Flights and trains into Prague all arrived at separate times, so we arranged to stay in the same hotel and meet for dinner. Next day, Mika took us on a tour of his capital city, bursting with pride whilst we froze to our bones. For once, the first one to complain was not Simone. It was me. The others understood the realities of minus 15° and dressed appropriately. Sure, I wore a thick coat, a beanie, gloves and sturdy boots. My jeans became so cold they stiffened into cardboard, chafing at each step. My nose and buttocks were numb and I was in desperate need of a warm drink. After ten minutes of my moaning, Mika took us to an underground bar, bought beers, hot chocolates and a peppermint tea for Simone. By the time I had thawed out, we were on the move again. Prague was pretty, at least what I could see of it between the tourists, with plenty of Gothic atmosphere. But way too perishing cold.

In the morning, we left for Mika's cabin in the forest. My disappointment about the castle was no longer an issue. When Mika first proposed we spent the change of millennium together in the Czech Republic at his family's place, I assumed he meant their aristocratic pile. I'd seen the pictures – online, Mikhael would never be so crass as to show off his family wealth. So when he explained his proposal was a holiday cabin at the lake, I had to call on all my thespian training to hide my disappointment. Dhan understood. Dhan always understood.

"What matters to us, Gael, is that we are together. Yeah, of course a Transylvanian castle would be a magic location, but ..."

"It's not Transylvanian, it's Bohemian."

"Whatever. The thing with the castle is we would be guests of Mika's family. On our best behaviour, trying to remember how to say thank you in Czech and not guzzling too much champagne. In the cabin, we will be on our own. We can cook, eat, drink and dance as much as we like. Best of all, we can get sweaty in the sauna, run through the snow and jump into the lake. Gael, this is gonna be the best New Year's Eve in living memory."

Dhan's deep brown eyes, simultaneously sincere and amused, gave me no choice but to capitulate. I let go of the castle.

"You'd better be right about that. Anyway, it's not the castle per se, just the chance to see how the other half live. I want to know how it feels to have staff, acres of land, horses and peacocks and corridors filled with fine art. Just for one weekend, I want to be a guest at a country house and enjoy the luxury of dressing for dinner."

He threw his head back, laughing and clapping his palms together. "You never got over Jane Austen, did you? I get it, Gael, I really do. We're in a world where everyone takes success for granted because they were born to it. In this particular Regency romance, you're the pretty maid with the fine eyes. Make no mistake, a handsome young sire shall spot you with your pert ways and pluck you from the flock. Thou shalt have a happy ending."

"And you?"

"Me? No roles for Brown Man with Big Mouth. Perhaps when Memsahib goes on a tour of the Empire, I can be Tubby Bloke in Turban fanning table with banana leaf. Talking of the Raj, do you fancy a G&T?"

On December 30, we departed Prague in Mika's minivan. The way I remember it, we left right after breakfast, but that's not possible because we didn't arrive till after dusk. The ambience was a mixture of trepidation and excitement. No one, not even Mika, knew exactly what to expect when the six of us would spend three days in the back of beyond. Sure, we'd spent last New Year's Eve together and the New Year's Eve before that, but those were at a club in one of Geneva's arty joints beside the Rhone and the first year university party on campus. There we were part of a crowd, able to mingle and mix, with the opportunity of simply leaving if we were not having fun. Not that any of us ever did. We stuck together, maybe dancing, flirting or conversing with someone else of our acquaintance, but always returning to sit with the group.

This time, it was different. We were closer, more of a unit than six individuals, and had no need of the herd. Where else would you want to spend the Millennium New Year's Eve but with your five best friends? In a castle, in a cabin, in a caravan, what did it matter? We wanted to celebrate such an event together in a conscious effort of making memories.

The drive to the cabin took almost two hours, through snowy rolls and folds of a landscape so uniformly white and blank, it was like driving through a gigantic duvet. We crossed bridges, spotted forests patterned with white-dusted pine trees, encouraged each other to admire the sunset, the only colour in the entire palette. Flakes of snow changed from hypnotic grey dots coming at us from the white sky to hypnotic white dots looming out of the dark blue night. The effect was like being in a spaceship whizzing through the stars.

Conversation had dried up along with the daylight and we travelled in silence. Mika and Lovisa rode up front, Clark and me in the row behind, our luggage between us. I glanced over my shoulder at the rear seats. Simone had fallen asleep on Dhan's shoulder. I couldn't see if he was awake or not.

Mika indicated and we left the main road to take a smaller lane into the forest. It had a light covering of snow and as far as I recall, we didn't see another vehicle pass in the opposite direction. The sense of being off grid and in the wilderness enveloped me, and I nudged Clark. We grinned at each other but said nothing.

"Here we go," said Mika, taking a still narrower lane into the trees. It opened out into a clearing, and a huge body of frozen water stretched away as far as I could see. The van came to a halt and we scrambled out, keen to get a look at our holiday home for the next three days.

Rustic, basic as hell and far smaller than I'd expected. Maybe I hadn't really got over the castle. Only three rooms, all with double beds, so immediately things were awkward. Mika and Lovisa took the master bedroom, as was their right. The two guest rooms were both a decent size but designed for couples. Clark and I were great mates and had previously exchanged bodily fluids, but I had no intention of letting that become a habit.

"I'm crazy excited to see the sauna," said Clark. Mika led us to the end of a corridor and opened the door. Inside was a pine-scented room with four wooden slatted loungers, assorted chairs and in the corner, a small interior room with a single black window. Clark and I opened the door and stuck our heads in. Two broad shelves, some kind of coal container and a wooden bucket with a ladle. I joined in with the oohs and aahs because it was, as Simone said, charmingly Nordic. It was also sinister as hell in that cabin-in-the-woods kind of way.

"Can I sleep in here?" asked Clark. "No offence, Gael, but I think both of us would be more relaxed in separate rooms. You know what, I really like the smell of this wood."

"You can sleep anywhere you like," said Mika. "Guys, I want you to be comfortable. I'll find some bed linen for Clark while the rest of you unpack. Then let's meet in the kitchen. Tonight, we're going local. Sausages, cheese, potato cakes and a few civilised beers. Because we're keeping our powder dry for New Year's Eve!"

Everyone bundled out of the door, enthused and delighted with our new quarters. Only Clark and I stayed behind.

I shuffled up to stand beside him and dropped my head against his shoulder. "Thank you," I said. "You're a decent man."

He tilted his head to rest it on mine. "Life is all about choices, sweetcheeks," he said. "May we always be free to choose. You know what, unpacking can wait. I fancy a Czech Pilsner and some of that stinking beer cheese. See, you're already glad we're not sharing a room." He planted a kiss on my forehead and with long strides, followed the others up the corridor.

We didn't go out that night. Where would we have gone? Mika and Lovisa prepared something not particularly memorable for dinner; we played games, drank strong Czech beer and stared at the fire while talking about what a change of the millennium might mean for us. We were all optimistic for the future, for each other, for the planet. Mellow, comfortable and happy to be together. Lovisa and I sat on a sheepskin rug, our backs to the sofa, arms entwined, laughing over her translations of Finnish Christmas songs. Dhan disentangled himself from Simone's octopus embrace and stood in front of the fireplace to give a speech, blathering on about new beginnings for all of us. He thanked Mika for providing the location, he thanked all of us for being the best mates he'd ever had and he thanked whoever brewed Czech Pilsner. The last thing I remember before I bade my friends goodnight was eating some kind of nutty, treacly pastry. No idea where it came from but it stuck my teeth together and I threw most of it into the fire. Everyone went to bed early. After all, we were saving ourselves for the start of the new millennium.

Chapter 2: Gael, 1999

Preparing for a party is often more fun than the party itself. Mika was up first, squeezing oranges and actually baking fresh bread. He had probably been for a jog beforehand as he had that pink, freshly scrubbed glow about him when he greeted us as one by one we wandered into the kitchen.

Breakfast was a leisurely affair, stretching over two hours and involving several pots of coffee. Other than our host, I was first up, followed shortly by Lovisa. No way could I lie in bed with such delicious smells of food wafting from the kitchen. We both pitched in, slicing bread, laying the table, frying bacon, scrambling eggs to serve ourselves, Simone, Dhan and eventually, Clark. By the time we'd finished eating and drinking it was 11:30 and time we got to work.

We formed three teams. Outdoors, kitchen duty and shopping. It seemed logical, if a little bit clichéd, that the outdoorsy, hiking, camping six-foot Alaskan Clark would help Mika with the wood chopping for the fire and cutting a hole in the ice. All of us were taken aback when Dhan volunteered to put on coat, boots and hat and go out into the snow with Mika instead. I assumed his motivation was the novelty value. The rest of us fell into line. There was no question Lovisa was in charge of the kitchen and her natural choice of sous chef would be Simone. The boys would work outside, leaving me to get the shopping, Dhan was right; I would never be more than the maid. We all sat at the kitchen table making a list of everything we would need for the next two days, threw fifty Koruna each into the kitty and set off to fulfil our respective duties.

I was looking forward to driving Mika's van and was just clearing the windscreen when Clark appeared by my side.

"Dhan and Mika have it covered. You shouldn't have to do this on your own. How about I give you a hand?"

"Said it before and I'll say it again, you are such a decent bloke. Is it OK if I drive?"

Everyone knew what a petrol head I was and he just gave an easy-going shrug. Even though the snow had stopped, it was the first time in my life I driven an unfamiliar vehicle in such unpredictable conditions. The journey to the main road was a white-knuckle ride. When we lurched onto clear, gritted tarmac, I realised I was sweating. I glanced at Clark, who was rolling a joint.

"Bet you wish you had driven now, right?"

"Nope. You handle this thing far better than I could. I'm just enjoying the ride."

"You liar. You're not going to light that in here, are you?"

"Depends on the rest of the drive."

The nearest town was forty minutes' drive on dodgy roads and I can honestly say it was one of the scariest experiences I've ever had behind the wheel. When we pulled up in the bleak, crowded car park, littered with dirty snow, we took an executive decision. Nerves shot by the journey, we deserved that joint.

Shopping in a Czech supermarket while slightly stoned is an experience I can truly recommend. Under fluorescent lights, faced with unfamiliar labels and strange faces, the whole thing felt like a hilarious dream. We overspent, much of it on chocolate, and sat in the van after we'd stowed our purchases, stuffing ourselves with the Czech equivalent of Twinkies. Clark offered to drive, but even after the stress of getting us here, my ego wasn't having that. On the ride back, the clouds cleared, leaving brilliant blue sky and sunshine sparkling off snow crystals. We didn't talk much, just uttered the occasional adjective.

"Awesome!"

"Beautiful."

"Stunning!"

"Unreal."

Back at the cabin, the atmosphere was skittish. Clark and I packed away all the food, accepted Lovisa's scolding for the items we'd forgotten, and with greater enthusiasm, accepted Simone's cheese and ham toasted sandwich. Dhan launched into a long and comic repetition of how his buttocks had frozen solid while setting lights in the snow. Mika explained these were necessary to guide us from the sauna to the lake, and conversation once again turned to the concept of getting sweaty and cooling off in freezing water.

If Simone's initial reaction to the idea was hostile, since seeing the lake she had vetoed the idea completely. Her arguments were reasonable. We would be drinking. Our judgements would be suspect. We didn't have Mika's family to guide us. We were miles from any kind of emergency assistance. Those who wanted to put themselves through the boiling sauna, icy water combination could have a cold shower. Or we could do the lake tomorrow, in daylight, sober. I think if it hadn't been for the issue of nakedness, she might well have persuaded us, at least the female half of the party. But as so often with our eclectic mix, the question of culture distracted us.

Dhan, who stood behind Simone's chair with his back against the kitchen sink, gazed out at the lake and already darkening forest. "I admit, I thought this was a wind-up. But after helping Mika cut the ice hole and fix the lights, I think he's serious."

"Of course I'm serious," said Mika. "I don't joke about

something like that. The sauna and dip is a family tradition. I would love to introduce my favourite foreigners to a genuinely Czech experience. But if you really cannot face jumping in the lake, as Simone says, the next best thing is a cool shower. It's not the same, but no one has to do this if you're too scared."

"Not scared, mate, just not prepared," Dhan laughed, his hands massaging Simone's shoulders. "I thought this was some kind of joke, so I didn't even bring my swimmers. That's why I can't go in."

Prankster, clown, sharp wit; Dhan's raison d'être was amusing people, so it was unusual to see him startled by the eruption of belly laughs at what he obviously considered a serious statement.

Lovisa was the first to recover. "You call that an excuse? It's a sauna, Dhan, no one wears swimming clothes. Everyone is naked."

"Naked!" Clark's head whipped around. "You're not serious."

Simone rolled her eyes and groaned. "And the uptight Anglo-Saxons strike again. What is the matter with you people? Why is the human body something to be ashamed of? Every summer in the south of France, I watched the Brits wriggling beneath their towels, terrified of exposing the smallest glimpse of skin. Why can't you be comfortable with your bodies?"

Lovisa and Mika were both laughing and nodding at Simone.

Mika spoke. "It's because Brits and Americans see naked bodies as nothing more than sexual vessels. They are incapable of taking off their clothes without thinking about sex. Europeans see nudity as a natural state. But then again, we don't have the sniggering, snorting attitude to bodily functions either." It was one of his favourite themes and one that got right up my nose. As international translators, all of us should know better than to deploy cultural stereotypes.

Dhan began to protest but Lovisa spoke over him. "We're all friends here. If getting naked makes you uncomfortable, you can wear your underwear. If Simone is afraid of the lake, she can use the shower instead. No one is under any pressure to do anything they don't want to do."

"I'm comfortable getting naked," said Clark, which came as a surprise to no one. He had a body he was rightly proud of and took every opportunity to display it.

Much as my loyalty to Dhan ran deep, no way was I going to be labelled an uptight Brit afraid of getting her kit off. "When in Prague …" I smiled. "Tonight I am going to strip off, get sweaty as hell, jump in the lake, and come back here for more of that stinking beer cheese."

Lovisa and Clark applauded. Mika's grin split his face. Simone reached her hand up to touch Dhan's, in a gesture of patronising reassurance. I knew that would drive him mad.

The evening meal concept was pot luck, as far as pot luck could be considered a highly organised tasting menu representing each of our home cultures. Once again, Lovisa had planned and executed the whole thing. The choices were bordering on cliché, but we told ourselves it was a sardonic nod to tradition. The main course was Mika's responsibility and a Czech classic: carp with potato salad. We opened with canapés of Alaskan smoked salmon with all the trimmings. Acknowledging his roots, Dhan chose a prawn pakora for the starter, followed by Simone's take on bouillabaisse. For dessert, Lovisa made classic Finnish star cookies and *glögg*, a kind of mulled wine. My lack of culinary ability was well known, so I could hear the collective sigh of relief when I volunteered to provide a cheeseboard. Not even I could screw that up.

Lovisa made her cookies while we were out shopping, and as salmon and cheese only needed taking out of the fridge, we left the kitchen to the others. Clark, Lovisa and I wrapped up in our warmest gear – Lovisa lent me a pair of leggings to wear under my sweatpants – and we went for a wander by the lake. The sun was sinking, but the sky was still cloudless and the afternoon light made everything slightly pinkish. We threw snowballs, ran in and out of the trees and made snow angels on pristine drifts. Breathless from racing each other back to the cabin and eager to get into the warm, we took a minute longer to stand at the door and soak in the scene.

Fir trees covered with a dusting of snow, the flat matt surface of the lake dully reflecting the blue of the sky and the last rays of the sun shining through the forest made for a scene so idyllic you wanted to either laugh or cry. I did neither, but took out my camera in a feeble attempt to capture the moment. The shutter had frozen solid. We bundled inside, out of the freezing air ready to party like it was 1999.

Chapter 3: Gael, 1999

The meal wasn't perfect, but pretty close. Dhan put a bottle of Moët et Chandon champagne outside the back door to chill and forgot about it. Simone's soup caught while she was trying to clear up the mess from the exploded bottle, so we called it Smoky Fish Soup and ate it anyway. Party pooper Mika kept trying to ration the alcohol – 'we must not be too drunk for the sauna and the lake!' – but not even Lovisa paid him any attention.

The fire blazed in the huge hearth and on the dining table, tea lights flickered in jars. We ate Clark's canapés standing around the fire, toasting each other's health and future with a glass of fridge-cooled champagne. Compliments flowed on how we all scrubbed up. The men all wore tuxedos and thanks to Simone and Lovisa's persuasion, all three women wore evening dresses. My camera now thawed out, we posed again and again in various combinations. A Night to Remember.

When we finally sat down to eat, there were more surprises. Each diner's setting was personalized with mini flags of each of our countries stuck into a bread roll; the brown paper place mats had been handwritten with text from a book or poem; a playing card served as a coaster and our wine glasses had individual identity rings. Lovisa had taken so much trouble to make the evening special to the six of us and her gestures touched every one of us. She was going to make a wonderful mama when she had children of her own, rather than five mildly dysfunctional peers.

So entertained were we by the perceptive bespoke settings, we barely noticed the burnt tang of the fish soup and declared ourselves a fan of the flavour.

Mika's place mat bore a passage from *The Unbearable Lightness of Being* by Milan Kundera. His eyes met hers with such softness, I had to look away. My wine glass ring had a double symbol: a gold star and the feminist symbol. I approved. When I saw Clark's, I laughed aloud. A tiny pair of Speedos – his favourite item of clothing. The Joker as Dhan's card could not have been more appropriate. I wondered who'd chosen for Lovisa.

"Me. I know myself best. Listen, the other side of everyone's mat is blank. Don't get it too dirty and we can all write a message for each other at the end of the meal. It will be a memory we can always keep, stains and all. Simone, that soup was lovely and now it's time for Dhan's starter. My glass is empty, Mika, my love."

He protested, she ignored him and poured herself a healthy measure of white.

Damn Dhan and his pakoras. Those floury little patties stuffed full of spicy prawns were dangerously moreish. I had two. Clark had three.

"Goddamn it, Dhan. You shoulda just put one on a plate with a little garnish. It's a starter, right? Shoving a pile of these in front of us just before the main course is asking for trouble."

"As if anything would ever spoil your appetite, Beer Hunter. If you're worried about the calories, I'll race you round the cabin before the main course." Dhan's eyebrows arched into perfect circumflexes, a look no one could resist. Even Mika shook his head with a grin, but scooped up the plate of patties and took it off the table. "I heard they're just as good cold," he said, removing temptation before he served the carp.

As soon as he was out of the room, Lovisa topped up all our glasses. Conversation turned to hopes and dreams again. This time not of a personal nature, but for the whole world. Where would we be in another ten years? Twenty? Thirty? Better off, surely. New geopolitical unions, commitments to a peaceful environment, neighbourly cooperation and greater appreciation of one another's strengths. Who am I kidding? Of course we were talking about ourselves as a metaphor for something larger. We were young and self-obsessed, what do you expect?

We ate pan-fried carp with potato salad and some greens I couldn't name and forgot to ask about until we were replete. Lovisa cleared the plates and suggested a respite before the next courses. The atmosphere grew more relaxed and comfortable, as we revisited in-jokes and old memories. Warm, well fed and full of wine, what kind of maniac would want to take off their clothes, get naked and sweaty, then jump into a lake?

Mika, that's who.

"It's nearly eleven. Those of us who want to do the sauna should start now. Fifteen minutes heat, run to the lake, jump in, run back and rest. Then we do it again."

Howls from me, Clark, Simone and Dhan.

"Do it twice?! No way, I'm only doing this once."

"I really think we should postpone this till tomorrow."

"Can't we just sit here and drink champagne?"

"You can, Dhan. But I'd like to heat myself until I'm melting, jump into natural freezing water and run into the house with my skin and circulation more alive than ever. This is how I want to start my millennium, 100% buzzing!"

He'd convinced me. Not just that, I was desperate to get out of that stiff dress. "I'm coming with you!" I shouted and rushed off to the spare room to strip off.

So it was that six pink people, only one wearing his pants, lay sweating on pine benches and inhaling the steaming air in a darkened wooden room. I didn't look at the others, just focused on my skin, my breath and coping with the heat. Dhan made a couple of wisecracks, but they fell flat. The ambience was not dissimilar to church.

A bell rang and Mika opened the door. "Take a robe and a pair of shoes. Follow the lights to the lake as quickly as you can. Wait till Simone attaches your safety band and then when I tell you, jump in. Please jump into the middle to avoid injury and keep your arms up above your head. Clark and I will pull you straight out again and Lovisa or Simone will wrap you in your robe. Please remember to put on your shoes immediately to protect your feet. Return inside the cabin and rest on one of the benches. Drink only water. When we are all ready, those who want to can do it again. It is a feeling like no other, that much I promise."

His words cut through my muggy mind and half-cut brain. Obey orders, or else. A fluffy green robe from the heater, a pair of chunky plastic flip-flops, and I followed the others out of the door. Steam rose from our bodies in a gauzy cloud. The night was surprisingly light as the moon shone its silvery blessing upon us. The ground illumination Dhan had complained so much about worked its fairy-tale magic, guiding us towards the water like magic luminous mushrooms.

I clung to Lovisa, half thrilled, half terrified and already feeling the icy air on my sweaty hairline. To my immense surprise, Simone attached a loop around her wrist, dropped her robe, stepped out of her shoes and jumped in first. She disappeared into the blackness and bounced back up with arms aloft, and the two men hauled her back onto the ice. Lovisa and I rushed to cover and cuddle her, thrusting her feet into her shoes. Next, Clark leapt into the water, emerging instantly with a whale-like gasp. Dhan and Mika fished him out.

Once dipped, we were supposed to go back to the house, but in spite of the bitter cold, we had to watch the rest of the gang. Lovisa went next, making fewer ripples than a knife and bobbing up with diver's arms aloft. Inspired by her cool composure, I asked Simone to attach my safety strap. I let the robe drop, stepped out of my flip-flops and stared at the dark hole in the ice. Every nerve in my body sounded alarms. *What's on the bottom? Will my feet get caught? Am I going to have a heart attack?* I shut all the voices down, placed my hands in prayer pose above my head and jumped.

Freezing water on hot skin feels like ants, electricity or a physical blow to the solar plexus. My skin was on fire and in an instant I was purified and clean. My first instinct was to gasp, but even in my shock, I knew that was a bad idea. My feet touched something reedy and I propelled myself directly upwards, where strong arms lifted me clear of the deep. Lovisa and Simone embraced me with a robe and slippers despite the fact a burning glow warmed me from within. Mika went next, in and out like a silverfish, barely requiring Clark's arm to emerge with a huge exhalation like a humpback whale.

We all turned to Dhan.

He held up his hands. "Not happening. Time out. Dhan and frozen lakes don't mix. First one back to the cabin is a cissy." He scuttled off, following the floor lights which led us all into the house.

Once indoors, Mika insisted we rest and listen to our bodies. We obeyed, reclining on the wooden slatted beds and after a few seconds of resisting temptation to chatter, observed what was going on. My blood, my internal organs, my skin were all having a party. Everything was alive and electric. I wanted to stay there forever, fizzing and glowing and saying cheers to every last bit of me, from toenails to earlobes.

Mika rose after about ten minutes and returned to the sauna. We duly followed and after a few moments, once we'd settled our naked bodies on various platforms, the door opened and in came Dhan.

"Bottled it, I know," he said. "Had a shower instead. Feels great, though, doesn't it?"

No one replied.

"You lot going back in?"

Lovisa lifted her head. "Whoever wants to go in again has everyone's support. Anyone who doesn't fancy the idea could start warming the *glögg* instead."

Dhan sat on the edge of the bench, still wearing his pants. Sweat dripped into my eyes, so I couldn't make out his expression. My head fell back onto my towel and I turned my attention to a more interesting conversation between me and my skin.

It was odd how soon nakedness became natural. When Mika stood up to open the door, his penis dangling, I didn't even get the urge to giggle. We all smiled and put on our robes, already excited about the jump. Dhan walked out of the sauna first, not turning left towards the bathroom, but opening the back door and striding into the snow.

"Dhan?" I asked.

"I'm not bottling this twice," he said.

Everyone applauded and I could feel the buzz before we even got outside. It was snowing again. We tramped down the path all the more grateful for the guiding lights at foot level.

When we got back to the ice-hole, Lovisa gestured towards me. "Gael, why don't you go first? When you're done, go back to the cabin and heat up the *glögg*. Is that fine with you?"

It was more than fine. I could hardly wait for that firey skin feeling again. With an uncharacteristic squeak of excitement, I threw off the robe and slippers and ran towards the hole. I didn't hesitate because I knew what to expect. But I had forgotten Mika's instructions to jump for the centre of the hole. My jump was too close and the edge of the ice scraped the back of my legs, bum and shoulder blades. The freezing water numbed the pain and only when I was replacing my robe did I feel the blood trickling down my legs.

"I scratched myself," I told Lovisa, as Dhan and Mika pulled Clark from the water.

She lifted the hem of my robe and I heard her gasp. "Go back to the house. Now. Forget about the *glögg*, I'll do it. As soon as we're done here, I'll come and get my first-aid kit. Don't be freaked out, it looks worse than it is."

She gave my shoulder a gentle push, so I did as I was told and made my way up the path, still exhilarated and alive, despite the stinging feeling across my shoulders.

Just before I opened the door, I looked behind me towards the circle of lights and the silhouetted figures beside the hole. I paused, curious to see if Dhan would actually go through with it. It was at that precise moment the lights went out. Simone shrieked, a male voice shouted something indistinct and there was a splash. Instead of laughter and applause, I heard nothing at all until Mika's voice released a loud curse. Everyone was calling Dhan's name, the panic in their voices sending a chill through me the weather could never match. I began running in the direction I had come only to be stopped short by Mika's shout.

"Gael! Get a torch, quick!"

Shaking so hard, I could barely turn the door handle, I entered the house and scanned the coat and boot racks. On the bottom shelf, there was a heavy duty rubber flashlight. I snatched it and with trembling fingers turned it on as I stumbled down to the lake to see only four people.

"What happened?" I shouted, my voice wobbling. "Where's Dhan?"

No one answered. Mika took the torch from me and shone the beam into the black hole. He walked in a circle, steady and methodical, using the light to scan the water. Clark got to his knees, sweeping an arm into the blackness. Simone repeated, "Oh my God, oh my God, oh my God," growing higher in pitch until Mika addressed Lovisa.

"Take her back to the house, call the police and an ambulance, get dressed and bring us some warm clothes. We'll keep searching. Gael, help her!"

We had to drag Simone away from the lake, all three of us shivering uncontrollably. Because Mika still had the torch and the guiding lights were extinguished, we couldn't see the path and lost our footing several times. We staggered inside, each shocked and numb with cold. Lovisa picked up the phone and dialled the emergency services. I dragged on some clothes, ran around collecting winter jackets and boots and left Simone standing by the fire, shivering and saying, "He wouldn't wait, I was trying to put it on, but he wouldn't let me, he just jumped, I had no time, it went dark and he just jumped in ..."

When I pushed open the front door, I heard a pop, rather like a champagne cork. Distant fireworks exploded into the sky, their colours blurred by the tears in my eyes. Far off bells were ringing as I blundered my way towards the two figures on the ice and I realised it had turned midnight. That was the start of the new millennium.

Chapter 4: Mika, 2001

Closure. I thought that as soon as we found the body, I would have closure. Don't tell my therapist, but part of me still thinks that might be true. The fact is, we didn't find him. Not that night, not the next day, not when the police trawled the lake after the thaw, not during that summer when I spent day after day after day snorkelling around the banks and diving into the depths. Without a body, we couldn't have a funeral. Without a body, we couldn't have a death certificate. Without a body, we couldn't say goodbye. It was absolutely ridiculous. Everyone knew he could not possibly have survived in water that temperature for much more than fifteen minutes, even without a solid sheet of ice above his head. Simone, clutching at straws, repeated over and over again what a strong swimmer he was. I bit my lip. He could have been a modern-day Mark Spitz but without somewhere to swim to, his fate was obvious.

To everyone's surprise, I passed my exams. Not the stellar grades my tutors had been predicting, but I did get my certificate as an international translator. I can't tell you how shitty that was. All the miserable crap that happened from January on – the blame from my friends, the shame of my family, the collapse of my relationship with Lovisa, the nervous breakdown – was all well deserved. Only when something good happened, such as achieving translator status, did I feel worse. The afternoon of our graduation ceremony, I hit a wall. Ducking out of the photographs and the champagne receptions, I went back to my apartment, swallowed every single sleeping tablet and painkiller I possessed and washed it all down with a genuine attempt at drinking a litre bottle of vodka.

It was Lovisa who saved me. Of course it was. Sometimes, I think she will always know when to reach out a hand. She was watching me and when I disappeared from what should have been one of the most triumphant days of my life, she knew something was wrong. She called my phone several times and on getting no reply, let herself in. Our split had been amicable and it didn't occur to me to ask her for the key back. She's never shared exactly what happened that day and I don't want to know the grim details. All I remember is waking up to find her sitting beside my hospital bed, her clean face as kind as a nun's.

In a way, Lovisa saved us all. She suggested the New Year's Eve memorial two years after Dhan's death. No one could have faced it before but once we had accepted the legal decision regarding his disappearance, something had to be done. We needed to mark it, to say our goodbyes. That wise Finnish female suggested London, Dhan's home. We could walk the streets where he grew up, try a curry in Brick Lane, prowl the markets and drink a pint of London Pride in a Soho ale house. I lost count of all the times Dhan's voice had taken us on a virtual tour of his home town. Finally, two years after his death, we were going to do it without him, to honour the memory of the man.

We were all raw and emotionally bruised after the previous twenty-four months, yet there were moments of lightness and laughter. I couldn't say that particular New Year's Eve was an unqualified success because we were all at different stages in the grieving journey, each taking small unsteady steps while scared to hold each other's hands. I had just begun to recover financially and as my bank balance crept up in tiny increments, my resentment, in equally tiny steps, started to fade.

We didn't go to Trafalgar Square to mingle with the drunken, excitable crowds. Instead, we walked the drizzly streets to London Bridge and watched the fireworks from the South Bank. Lovisa unzipped her rucksack and handed each of us a miniature bottle of sparkling wine. I hesitated, after being dry for seven months, and unscrewed the cap. After all, this was for Dhan. The bells rang, the whoops echoed across the river and the fireworks began. We raised our bottles, yelled 'to Dhan!' and drank. We hugged each other, some tearful, some peaceful, and stood in silence watching colours fill the sky.

The next day we walked in Greenwich Park, taking photos and talking with more ease than had been possible for many months. Underfoot, frosted blades of grass crunched beneath our boots and our breath made clouds in the air.

Gael linked her arm into mine and Simone's. "We should do this again," she said. "Not every year, we've got our own lives to lead. Why not every other? To tell the truth, I wasn't initially convinced by Lovisa's idea. But it did me good, even if I speak only for myself."

"Me too," Clark agreed and we all murmured some kind of assent.

"So how about doing this again in 2003? We'll go somewhere nice together, catch up with each other's lives, celebrate the New Year and remember Dhan."

"That's a lovely thought," said Simone, her pretty nose red with cold. "We should never forget him or our friendship. Also I would do anything to have a valid excuse to have a break from my family over the Christmas season."

As newly independent graduates, we all agreed with that sentiment. And so it began. A New Year's Eve tradition; both benediction and curse.

Chapter 5: Lovisa, 2003

Kefalonia was probably the first time each of us spent the New Year celebrations actually celebrating. It was the five of us, same as last time, but much less painful. Of course the grief was in the foreground, but the foundations were stronger. Each of us was happier and more stable than the last time we had met. I was able to see Mika without feeling that desperate loss which made us both miserable. More than all of those things, Simone's choice of location worked its magic.

I had read *Captain Corelli's Mandolin*, and I expect you have too. Louis de Bernières's novel talks about the light, the quality of limpid air and the peculiar softness it lends the landscape. That year, we were all earning decent salaries and decided to book a villa, rather than hotel rooms. I couldn't wait to escape the Northern European winter to enjoy some sun, sand and optimism.

It was exactly as I hoped. We walked along cliffs and beaches, ate outside traditional cafés, teased each other and marvelled about how far we had come in three years. It was that time of our mid-twenties when we thought we had arrived at adulthood. Youthful energy fuelled us, and of course informed us, but ignorance is bliss. The combination of achievement and endless potential struck me hard while spending time with this group of people. The inspirational feeling of power, the dominance over life, all the successes still to be experienced. Looking forward. We'd earned it, hadn't we? The thought of Dhan's potential crossed my mind on more than one occasion, tempering my optimism for the future.

Kefalonia was running on a small flame. Just locals and a select bunch of tourists, either die-hard fans of the Greek island or groups with an agenda like ours, inhabited the local bars and restaurants which had not closed for the winter. The touristy part wasn't of interest anyway, and the calmness of Greek-style towns had something magical. The masses had abandoned the island, but those who remained shared an even closer bond. That included strangers like us. All that counted was being here, now.

One afternoon, we collected some driftwood and made a fire on the beach. We grilled seafood, brought some salads and flatbreads, and drank rough red wine, while watching the sun sink into the sea. The chill of the evening crept over us and although Gael and Clark dragged more wood onto the flames, I grew cold.

Using a need for the bathroom as an excuse, I stuffed all our Tupperware and aluminium cooking trays into one big bag and trudged up the sandy path in the direction of our villa. A brisk breeze ruffled my hair as my toes squished into the white sand. By the time I got to the top, I was breathing hard and took a break. I stared out at the sea, inhaling the restorative powers of the ozone and looked up at the stars. Never one of those people to believe dead relatives are twinkling down at me from a long distant planet, I didn't feel it was an emotional moment. At least, not from the perspective of the one event that connected all five of us.

Inside the villa, all was silent and dark. I lit citronella mosquito candles before putting on the lights. In the kitchen, I was running hot water to clean our greasy tableware when the French windows opened and Gael came in, her face glowing from the afternoon's sun. She grinned at me and switched on the stereo and the sound of the Red Hot Chili Peppers filled the room with energy.

Moving with the beat, we cleaned all the crockery and cutlery, washed up the glasses and replaced everything back in the cupboards. We took the remnants of a bottle of red wine onto the terrace to wait for the others returning from the beach.

"Today has been wonderful," I said. "For me, the pain is still there. Perhaps it will never leave. But it's not as all-consuming as it was two or three years ago."

We stared out at the restless ocean, allowing its ebb and flow to soothe us. "You're right. It gets easier and a location like this helps. Great choice by Simone. The funny thing is, Dhan would have loved it here. I can just imagine him getting all excited about building a fire on the beach, can't you?"

"Hmm."

Gael looked at me sideways. "What is it?"

I'm not sure what provoked it but I wanted to tell someone. "My counsellor suggested that kind of thinking is not helpful to me. Projecting what Dhan would have liked, or hated, or whatever. I'm not criticising you, just stating my own situation."

"Right." She was silent for a while. "Why does your counsellor think it's unhelpful?"

"What I have begun to realise is that there are two different kinds of Dhan. There is the imaginary, perfect version of the man he should have become. The wonderful father to Simone's baby, the caring husband, the loyal friend, the life and soul of every party. Then there is the real Dhan. Our memories of that young man are filtered through the tragedy. We recall a joker, a comedian, a good friend who sometimes did bad things. I've only recently acknowledged this to myself and later shared it with my counsellor. She advised me to start with forgiveness."

She exhaled. "We forgave each other a long time ago, Lovisa. It was not our fault."

"I'm not talking about forgiving ourselves. Where I need to start is by forgiving Dhan."

"Forgive Dhan? For jumping?"

"No." I spoke in a rush, keen to get it all out before the others returned. "When we went to Prague, I was a seething mass of fury. I didn't show it because it wasn't anyone else's problem but Dhan's." I took a huge inhalation of night air, memories tightening my chest.

Gael must have sensed a story brewing, so emptied the bottle into our glasses, sat back and listened.

"You and Simone were fluent so you weren't in the French tutorials. Together, the five of us only ever spoke English. You probably don't remember how poor Dhan's French was but I can promise you, he was dreadful. After he failed his first year, he had to pass the first semester of our second year, otherwise he was out. He asked me to coach him. Dhan was not a good student and I became frustrated with his laissez-faire attitude. To be fair, he saw me as a girly swot and thought I should loosen up a little. If it had been only that, a difference in attitudes to study and education, it would never have been a big deal. I know I'm a girly swot, I can live with that."

I noticed a small pile of tissues growing beside my wine glass. My fingers were shredding one of the napkins I'd brought back from the beach.

"Girly swots are like tortoises. They get there in the end," said Gael.

It was a weak effort but it came from the heart. I gave her a smile. "I don't suppose anyone else was aware of the details. After all, we're talking over four years ago. Monsieur Rochat rejected my French paper at the end of that term. He could have failed me on French for that semester, but he gave me the opportunity to present something else before the end of the year. That's why I had to spend every spare minute over Christmas translating a completely different text. Two days before we flew to Prague, I faxed him my paper. He accepted it and gave me a B grade. That one mistake dragged down my whole average."

Gael shook her head so vigorously, her earrings waggled like puppy tails. "No way! Rochat rejected one of your papers? I'm sure I'd have remembered that. You were his favourite, a shining example of the perfect translator. What the hell did you do wrong?"

I stared out across the moonlit water as a burst of laughter reached us from down at the beach. "Nothing. I did nothing wrong. Someone else had submitted the exact same paper three days before. I was accused of plagiarism and would be penalised with a fail grade unless I submitted an original piece before the end of the year." My face flushed as I relived the embarrassment. I faced her, willing her to understand.

The tumblers finally fell into place. "Holy shit! Dhan stole your work?"

"Yes. Dhan stole my work. It wasn't difficult. He knew my lecture timetable and when I was in the library or at Mika's place. All he had to do was ring the bell and say he'd come to see me. One of my housemates would let him in. He copied my work verbatim, complete with the mistakes I corrected in the final draft."

"And you didn't tell Monsieur Rochat? He knew what a lazy sod Dhan could be. We all did. But to copy your work and drop you in it? That's unconscionable."

"Would you like some tea? Or another glass of wine?" I went into the kitchen without waiting for a reply, filled with an urgent need to move, to pace and break the tension. There were no more wine bottles open, but we did have a bottle of port. I made a pot of peppermint tea and filled two liqueur glasses with ruby port. It didn't look ruby red, cherry red or scarlet, but the blackish red of arterial blood.

"Here we go. Tea and port instead of wine. No, I didn't tell Rochat, although he gave me the opportunity to explain. At first,

I went looking for Dhan, to confront him and force him to confess, but he'd already gone home for Christmas. He left me no choice but to redo the paper. I was so angry and hurt; I swear I could have killed him."

Gael stared at me, her expression outraged. "Dhan must have known he'd be putting you in an impossible position. Either you took the hit or you exposed him as a plagiarist. He counted on your honour and human decency to save his skin. Bloody hell, Lovisa. One shouldn't speak ill of the dead, but what a shitty thing to do."

I had no answer to that and sipped my port.

"So when we met in Prague was the first time you'd seen each other since you found out what he'd done?"

The port was sweet and thick in comparison to the wine, but perfectly drinkable. I closed my eyes, picturing the scene. We were taking photographs as we crossed the Charles Bridge in Prague and noticed we had lost the others. That was my moment to challenge him.

"He laughed, Gael. He actually laughed. He said he knew it was, and I quote, 'a bit cheeky', but that my grades were so good, one failed paper wouldn't do me too much harm. I tried to explain the impact that could have had on my career if I hadn't spent my Christmas working on a new submission. He applauded me and said he knew I'd pull something out of the bag. He didn't care. So long as his arse was covered, I could go whistle." My voice cracked a little and I wished I hadn't shredded that napkin.

We sat there for a long time in silence, gazing out to sea but our minds on the past. Voices drew closer, giggling and singing.

"Sounds like they finished the wine," I smiled.

Gael reached out to rest her hand on mine. "Thank you for trusting me with this and I'm sorry you had to go through such a crappy experience. Your counsellor is right. You have to forgive him, but in your shoes, that would take me a very long time.

You're a good person, Lovisa."
    I wasn't.

Chapter 6: Clark, 2005

2005 was a very different celebration because I was the organiser and we were going to Berlin. I was looking forward to it way more than I had anticipated Kefalonia. The language was not an issue; I spoke German with confidence, if not 100% accuracy. The key element that excited me was a city break for young people in a vibrant place, not another granny tour of an island. Sure, Dhan is dead. But we're not. We're alive and about to embark on a whole new twelve-month of chances. New Year's Eve should be an opportunity for hope and optimism, and letting go of the past. And if that includes nightclubs, dancing, drinking and probably narcotics, so much the better.

The second thing I introduced that year was the plus ones. If we only ever focused on the five of us and the missing number six, we would never move on. I suggested inviting significant others, mainly because I wanted to squeeze every last drop of joy from Juanita. Women like her never stick around for long. At first it's intense, passionate and they're all over you. Then they get bored and move on to the next adventure without even a backward look. That's why I wanted to include strangers this time around. No one responded to my suggestion. I thought the idea was dead in the water until Gael invited her sister. Yes! Dynamics – all change.

Man, Berlin is something else. There's an anarchic undertone to the efficiency of the place, a sense that anything could happen. Not surprising, I guess, for a city divided and reunited. Sixteen years after the wall fell, traces of its presence remained in a physical sense. But what of the people? Loved ones, friends and neighbours separated for years, until one night, the distance was removed. How do you adapt to such a monumental change? After the first flash of excitement disappeared, the adjustment can't have been easy. People change while they are apart, coping with altered circumstances, growing used to the freedom, or lack of it. When people develop at different speeds, sudden reunification must come as a shock to both sides. I guess some people asked themselves if it was wise to expect two countries to become one overnight. Reunions aren't always a happy occasion.

We avoided the tourist sights and hung out at quirky little art galleries and bars with live music. Gael's sister, Orla, was a real shot in the arm, always proposing a detour to see a work of graffiti, some street performers or a poetry slam. We ate at a *Bierkeller* and hit the nightclubs till three in the morning, when we bought donuts as we wandered home. Juanita was an incredible dancer with such enthusiasm for life, she hypnotised everyone she met. The addition of two new faces to our group worked like seasoning in the soup. Seven was even better than five.

On New Year's Eve, we cooked dinner together in the huge apartment I'd rented. Then we went out into the streets, wishing everyone a *Guten Rutsch* into the New Year. We counted down to midnight and danced in one of the squares. Later we split up. The party people, me, Juanita, Mika and Orla, wanted to go clubbing. The girls weren't crazy about the idea and I was in no mood to persuade them. Trying to keep everyone happy is a thankless task. Simone's sour expression had pushed me to the end of my tether over the last two days. Several times I asked myself why we bunch of misfits were doing this again, when I could be perfectly happy without them.

My point is, people grow. We were in our late teens when we met and over those three years, yeah, we formed a bond stronger than most. I reckon had Dhan not died that night, we would all have drifted apart. It's only natural, you know? Maybe seeing each other once in a while, the gaps between getting longer, the quality of experiences getting poorer, until the physical connection just dried up. We could still keep up with each other's lives via the sanitised version presented to social media. No guilt about a friendship gone fallow. Just the illusion of closeness with the reassurance of distance. Who wouldn't sign up to that?

Maybe not all of us. Lovisa is our 'Mom', keeping our five-way relationship alive like an artificial lung. Birthdays, successes, moves, failures and love affairs all merit a reminder or a message. Without her, the connection would wither and die, like fresh-cut flowers in a cemetery.

Like all moms, she has her favourite. No one can deny that's Simone. A favourite child earns her place through sweet-natured charm or helplessness. Simone uses the latter. Always needy, confused, fretful and vulnerable, Simone plays every trick in the book to make us all come running to her aid. Everyone falls for it, except me. Even Gael tolerates her shtick, but I reckon she sees through the act. How come Simone, as the local, couldn't cope with one single practical action required for registration at university without one of us holding her hand?

The woman is pretty, that much is true. Heads turn when she enters a room. But she's like dragon fruit. Appealing exterior, apparently packed with stuff that's good for you, but the inside is bland. Maybe even a little sour on second bite. She's manipulative and sly, playing people against each other. Classic youngest sibling behaviour, according to Gael, who should know. If that is not enough of a deterrent, I'm here to warn you, my friends, she's the worst kind of European snob.

It's a well-honed instinct I've developed to a high degree of precision, as an American expat. Or to look at it through their eyes, an immigrant. That sense of when I'm being judged. The glance from head to foot, zoning in on whatever displeases them most, the false smile, the compliment on how good my French is (with silent follow-up clause) ... *for an American*. The use of Swiss French slang to exclude me.

Yeah, been there, done that, got *le T-shirt*. I made up my mind to be civil to Simone but give all her negative crap a wide berth. Then what happens? She starts dating my flatmate. I come home, she's there, draped around him like a *foulard*. The two of them on the sofa, her legs over his, her arm behind her head to lift her chest just so. And of course the nights. Noises of endless lovemaking. So irrelevant when you're involved. So utterly disturbing when you're forced to listen.

"Hi, Clark! If you're hungry, we made cheese soufflés. There's plenty left in the kitchen."

You can stick your soufflés, lady, I thought. "Just eaten, guys, but thanks," I said.

As for Dhan, he was under some sort of spell. On one of the rare occasions she wasn't at our place, I asked him if he thought this fling had long-term potential. My timing wasn't great. He was trying to reboot his computer and kinda distracted.

"Simone? No way. Too high-maintenance. What is wrong with this OS? Should have called it POS." He scratched his head and then noticed I was still standing there. "No, mate, it's just sex and a bit of variety. And when she gets the kit on, the fun begins ..." His whistle turned into a frown as he glared at the screen. "Forty minutes to restart? They have got to be joking."

I could see his mind wasn't on our conversation, so left it there.

A couple days later, I was heading toward campus in brilliant sunshine, gazing up at the mountains on the other side of the lake. Days like this, I couldn't believe my luck. How long had I hoped to study languages in a cosmopolitan European city? Right here, right now, I was living the dream. Lac Leman reflected the mackerel-pattern of wispy clouds, filling me with an irrational joy. Something about water attracted me. Lakes, the ocean, rivers, whatever, I loved them all. I ran through my languages. *L'eau, el agua, das Wasser* and hesitated. Was it *das* or *der Wasser*? I should have known something that basic by now. Reminded of my intention to get some kids' books out of the library to work on my German, I quit gazing at the lake and headed for the university.

Out of nowhere, Dhan appeared at my elbow. "Hey, big man, you got half an hour?"

His grin and bright eyes told me he was up to something. Time and time again, he would try to persuade me to cut lectures, skip a class and join him for a beer, a boat trip or some other thrill-seeking opportunity. Dhan was pretty hard to refuse.

"Depends. I don't have to be anyplace till four, so I was on my way to the library."

"The library? We can do better than that. Come shopping with me. I need your advice."

He placed his hand on my shoulder and guided me off the university grounds. We took a bus a couple stops, Dhan talking non-stop about a comedy show he'd seen the night before and got off at Monthoux, at the heart of the Pâquis district. He led me up a side street I didn't know, beckoning me to follow. Pâquis, like all European red-light districts, is a mixture of cool and scuzzy. This particular corner was definitely at the scuzzy end, with strip clubs and lap dancing joints every twenty metres. Dhan stopped and pointed. "Here we go!"

A sex shop. In the window, some PVC gimp suits which would give you an infection by just looking at them. I stopped, an uncomfortable tension in my shoulders. This was all wrong.

"And we're coming here why, exactly?"

"For some kit. Simone's Valentine's present to me was a

promise she'll wear whatever costume I buy for her. That's why I need your advice. My imagination is a bunch of soft-porn clichés so I'm leaning to the saucy French maid. Can you imagine, with her accent?"

My stomach turned toxic and I tasted bile at the back of my throat. "Sorry, man, this is not my scene. Not my scene at all. Maybe if you're shopping for kinky outfits to spice up your sex life, you should take your girlfriend." I spun on my heel and speed-walked my way out of there. Dhan's voice called after me but I didn't, couldn't turn around. What the hell was he thinking?

Maybe the reason I was recalling all that shit at six-thirty in the morning after three hours' sleep was because I could hear people having sex. After tumbling out of a nightclub and getting a cab back to the Berlin apartment, Juanita and I fell into bed sometime after three am, in the words of The Dead Kennedys, too drunk to fuck. It was obvious to everyone that Orla and Mika were going to get it on and I was happy for him. For both of them. But the sounds of passion from the room next door in the pre-dawn darkness took me back to that small room in Geneva, listening to squeals and moans, clenching my fists and curling my toes, my pillow pressed over my head. That knot in my stomach returned for the first time in years.

Even though I couldn't admit it back then, a part of me knew that feeling. As the man who'd slept with pretty much half of the people in our year and some above and below, I had a reputation. But on hearing my flatmate and his girlfriend role-playing master and servant, I was jealous.

Chapter 7: Simone, 2007

I have no idea what I would have done without Lovisa. She has been there for every significant event in my life since 1997. How I managed before we became friends I no longer recall. It is bizarre to think we met just ten years ago, so deeply woven together are our lives. True, not many people have been through so much so young. The death of my lover and her friend, my terminated pregnancy, Lovisa's split with Mika, our graduation, our shared flat as we started our careers. She was a witness at my wedding and a shoulder to cry on through the divorce. The sister I always wanted. My biological sisters, both older than me, are superficial and selfish. I don't think they care about anyone else but themselves, although they are on very good terms with the bathroom mirror.

The biennial New Year's Eve gatherings were Lovisa's idea. Even though I resented the concept of sharing my grief as the anniversary loomed, their company comforted and reassured me. In 2003, in Kefalonia, we had laughed more than we cried. For a Swiss, there's something magical about an island. In spite of the fact it was too cold to swim, we spent most of our days on the beach. The sunshine, the sea and the extraordinary light acted as a therapeutic treatment, lifting us all, smoothing out wrinkles and focusing our attention on the present rather than the past. We were, as they say, in the moment.

Berlin in 2005 was not as much fun. The presence of two strangers made me uneasy, and drugs cause me problems. Clark has always been an experimenter with pharmaceuticals. Perhaps he is searching for something to make him happy. Personally, I don't like losing control. In addition, if everyone around me is stoned or high or whatever they call it, I am excluded. Then Gael's overbearing sister hooked herself on to Mika and the party split into singles and doubles. On top of all of that, I dislike German food.

Another thing that spoiled the trip for me was Mika having a one-night-stand. I thought he was better than that. We all know Clark cannot keep it in his trousers, but Mika? Very disappointing behaviour. It didn't seem to bother Lovisa, or if it did, she hid it well. I often wondered why she hadn't tried to repair their relationship. On a positive note, I knew his interest in casual sex meant he wasn't seeing anyone seriously. Mika's not the kind of guy to cheat on a girlfriend.

2007 should have been Gael's turn to organise the New Year event except that we all met up in September for our Ten-Year University Reunion. I was reluctant to attend, despite the fact Lovisa and I were the only two people in our year who did not have to travel. Reunions are basically a competition. Who has succeeded best, aged well and achieved the most? Everyone compares, compliments and after the event, criticises. I was not looking forward to it at all. To tell the truth, I was dreading every minute. As it turned out, I should not have concerned myself, because Lovisa was there.

For the first few years after university, Lovisa and I had shared an apartment. When I decided to buy a place, she moved further out of Geneva to save money. That first apartment I owned was small but large enough to accommodate a guest in my study. Lovisa's place was bigger, but too far out of the city for me. Because she had a spare room and a sofa bed, she offered two places to stay, first come, first served. My relationship with

Clark had never been easy and Gael tended to drink more than made me comfortable, so I reached out to Mika. Just a friendly gesture. He thanked me but said he'd already booked a hotel so he could get some work done. So I went out to buy a dress instead.

The five of us agreed on a pre-reunion apéro, sitting in Lovisa's living room, browsing through photographs and reminding each other of our classmates' names and related scandals. We drank cocktails and hypothesised about the evening ahead. Lovisa looked stunning in a black velvet dress with long gloves and a gauzy cape, her blonde hair piled high. The other three wore black tie, including Gael. While I understood the refusal to conform to gender stereotypes, I cannot say her curvy body shape is ideal for the sharp lines of a suit. My own dress was vintage Dior in champagne-coloured silk, and I borrowed my sister's diamonds, a Cartier necklace and earrings to catch the light.

The look on Mika's face told me everything I needed to know. Not only would I be the best-dressed woman in the room, but also the most popular, surrounded by genuine friends. The evening ahead began to seem less of a chore. We toasted each other with Cosmopolitans and took a taxi to the venue, a hotel on the lake. The evening was quite lovely. Even in late September, it was warm enough to sit on the terrace. I drank champagne, embraced old friends, accepted compliments, asked polite questions and even danced a couple of times. Gael hardly sat down, twirling, jitterbugging and demonstrating her skill at Irish dancing. She looked like she was having enormous fun and every time I saw her, I had to smile.

As the party began to wind down, Lovisa and I found a table on the terrace and Gael managed to source an unopened bottle of Piper-Heidsieck. Tired and happy, we sat there grinning at each other and the lights of Geneva reflected in the water.

"You were great fun this evening," I told Gael. "Really the life and soul of the party."

Lovisa agreed. "You were. It must be a British thing. To me, your energy fills a void."

We paused for a moment, considering the word 'void'. It could have dampened the scene but then Gael spoke.

"Thank you. I had a ball. OK, so I didn't pull but the night is still young and I have already asked what time the barman gets off work. Looks like Clark got lucky with that Danish Glamazon. He's punching above his weight there, but good luck to him."

Gael and Clark were constantly pursuing sex. Neither seemed to have an agenda other than simply getting laid. I shook my head, curious at why it seemed so important to them. I looked back at the hotel ballroom, emptier now as people left or moved on to the after parties. Mika, usually easy to spot in a crowd, was nowhere to be seen.

"Where's Mika? Did he leave already?" I asked, with a yawn.

Gael shook her head. "Typical bloody Mika. He's sitting in the corner talking shop with some equally boring men. Lovisa, you've probably noticed already, but Bernadette – the redhead in the jumpsuit – told me she has the mad hots for Mika. Should I tell her to lay off?"

Lovisa lifted her head and laughed, releasing her hair from its clip. "Of course not! My relationship with Mika is history, but I still love him, as I love all of you. I want him to be happy. He should have fun, dance, laugh, have sex. God knows, somebody should. I'm not exactly setting the world on fire."

I laughed, but guilt dragged at the corners of my mouth. Mika had ended their relationship because of me. In my grief and panic in the first weeks of 2000, I was hopeless at anything practical. That was why I carried Dhan's baby for sixteen weeks, despite knowing I was in no condition to have a child. Lovisa arranged the termination and ensured I attended all the subsequent counselling. Mika's Catholic conscience couldn't stand that. All the cracks after Dhan's death, the inquest and the grim months of uncertainty gradually mended, but mine and Lovisa's decision to abort an unwanted pregnancy shattered their relationship into a thousand pieces.

"Nor me," said Gael. "I don't usually make New Year's resolutions, but this year, I am determined to have more sex."

"What happened to that Dutch woman you liked?" I asked. "She sounded perfect for you."

"Marieke? She was perfect for me. Sexually speaking, 2006 was a vintage year, what with her in Amsterdam and Stefan in Brussels. He was the classic office romance, editor of the paper, with that kind of sexy intelligence I can't resist. Snogging in the lift, knee-tremblers over the desk, the whole nine yards. Then they both went back to their wives."

"I'm sorry," I said. Gael's attitude always surprised me. She never looked at the menu and made a considered decision. She treated love as fast food, snatched when she was hungry and the waste discarded.

"I'm not. Hot sex for a good seven months with a fit woman and a steamy three-month liaison with the boss? Here's to 2008 bringing plenty more where that came from!"

We bounced our flutes against each other's and repeated her wish, then fell silent amid the noise of revellers cheering as they left the hotel. My questions itched at me and in the relaxed, companionable mood, it seemed fair to ask.

"Gael, you don't have to answer this if you don't want to, but I'd like to understand how you identify. Do you describe yourself as bisexual? Or are you straight but curious about lesbianism? Or vice versa? It doesn't matter either way; I'm just trying to understand how you see yourself."

Gael gave me a fond smile. "Our Simone, the Queen of Putting Things in a Box. How do I identify? As not bloody fussy. Cheers, girls!"

The next day, I got up late and spent a good half an hour on my toilette before taking the tram to Lovisa's place. The plan was to have breakfast with the rest of the party. Only Gael and Lovisa were at the apartment. Clark had not returned the night before and we exchanged knowing looks. Mika was not answering his phone, so perhaps the redhead had succeeded. I tried not to mind. If Lovisa could accept it, so should I.

Gael made coffee and Lovisa made *Pannukakku*, or Finnish pancakes and we went out into the sunny autumnal streets of Geneva. We walked through the old town, as far as Place de Neuve and the Parc des Bastions, where we spent so many hours as students. The trees were changing colour and the weather fresh. We wandered through colonnades, between the giant chessboards and along the Reformation Wall reminiscing about who had done what, with whom and where.

"Remember when the three of us went to the Berlin Wall? Those useless men couldn't get out of bed that morning either. But that wall was a humbling sight."

Lovisa, her pure face sad as she surveyed the tourists taking photographs, lifted her shoulders to her ears. "I remember. It touched all three of us. A scar across a city, a country. Scars aren't always bad. Sometimes, they act as a reminder, a lesson learned. Not that Berlin could ever forget."

I shivered a little and drew my scarf closer. We walked on to the lake, each wrapped up in our thoughts.

"Gael? Can I ask you a question?"

"Is it about my sex life again?"

I smiled and shook my head, wondering if I really wanted to raise this, here and now. "No. This is not about sex."

"Then fire away, madame. What do you want to know?"

I tried to keep my tone light. "That night. The second time you jumped in the lake, you hurt yourself, no? The backs of your legs got scratched. Did that leave a mark?"

Gael's smile faded as she thought about it. "No, it was only a graze." She bumped her shoulder against Lovisa. "I remember you telling me it looked worse than it was and as ever, you were right. Backs of my legs, bum and shoulder blades scraped the ice, but no worse than falling over on tarmac. It healed far faster than the other stuff."

I didn't need to ask what 'the other stuff' meant.

Lovisa shook her head. "I recall there was a lot of blood, which made things much harder to explain when the police arrived. We were so very stupid."

She linked her arms into ours and we proceeded along the promenade like a wall of our own, cemented by mutual affection.

My regard for these two women led me to continue. "You know, I have a scar."

"A scar from that night?" asked Gael.

"Or do you mean emotionally?" Lovisa asked, her voice gentle.

Without warning, my throat swelled and I stopped, tears seeping from under my tightly shut lids. I tried wiping them away with my gloves, but more took their place. Gael brushed maple leaves from a park bench and we sat, me in the middle.

I didn't attempt to speak. I took off my gloves and simply unbuckled my watch strap stretching my right arm towards them. Just below my wrist, there were two white marks, like tadpoles swimming up my forearm. Lovisa held my hand, her head tilted in enquiry.

I spoke in stilted bursts, trying to swallow more tears. "Those marks were made by Dhan's fingernails. When he came to the ice hole, I tried to stop him. He didn't have a safety band so I caught his right arm and pulled him back. He was wet, sweaty and I couldn't get a strong grip. He tore my hand away. He *tore* it as if we were fighting. He dug in his nails and crushed my hand to get me off him. Afterwards, the bruising was ugly, but in comparison to other traumas, I hardly noticed. The scars from where his nails cut deep are still there. I can't understand why he did that."

I gulped and replaced my watch. They both leaned in close to comfort me.

"OK," said Lovisa. "Let's say he *was* fighting. Not you. His fear. He finally decided he couldn't miss out, grabbed his courage and decided to jump into the lake before he could change his mind. You tried to prevent him going through with it and in his panic or exhilaration, he didn't realise how rough he was."

"That's possible," Gael agreed. "You have such delicate skin, you bruise like a peach if I as much as poke you in the arm." She poked me in the arm.

I couldn't smile. "You didn't see his face, Gael. At that moment, he hated me."

"Look, I'm not defending the stupid bastard. He jumped in like a madman and ended up dead. We all know this was on Dhan."

"Yes, it was. What I am trying to say is that it was more than a moment of intoxication. He was so determined, so ruthless ... oh, I can't explain. You weren't there."

Gael's face closed down and she took her arm from my shoulders.

I reached out and touched her coat. "I'm sorry, that's not fair, I meant ..."

Lovisa slid her gloved hand into mine. "Simone, we'll never know what was in his mind that night, and trying to guess his reasoning only prevents us from moving on. We're still getting over what happened, because it was only seven years ago. Moments like this surprise us when we least expect it and are more likely to recur when we're all together. We understand. Now, my backside is frozen. Let's go find a coffee shop to warm ourselves up. What do you say, Gael?"

Gael bounced to her feet. "I say bollocks to a coffee shop. I want to find an old-style wine bar and drink a bottle of their cheapest vintage." She offered a hand to pull me to my feet. "Come on, let's go local, drink white wine and eat an obscene amount of cheese. It's the only way to treat a hangover."

In January, I got the chance to work as a simultaneous interpreter at the United Nations, covering someone's paternity leave. The job I'd always wanted. There was no way I was letting that get away. I worked like a crazy person, reading all the background material, studying the speakers' styles, meditating to improve my concentration and being unforgettably charming to everyone in the department. It worked. Three months later, the head of translations offered me a full-time position and suggested we might try a few positions of our own. I accepted the job but demurred on the affair, citing my husband. I didn't mention the divorce and still wore my wedding ring. Women in particular tended to relax when they thought I was married and it had the added advantage of putting men off. Not all; some saw it as a challenge.

All I wanted was a nice place to live and a job at which I excelled. Men only messed things up. Anyway, romance was the last thing on my mind. In my life, I had only ever loved one person and that would never change.

Chapter 8: Clark, 2009

Ten years. It was always going to be a weird one. I toyed with the idea of giving the occasion a miss, as I've only been married a year and quite like hanging out with my wife. To be honest, I'm pretty damn sure that some of my friends blame far too much of their current dysfunctional behaviour on the death of a friend ten years earlier. Perspective, people, you know? At some stage, we're all going to have to move on with our lives. Some of us already have.

Cass knows about the tradition and why it started. Because she is the coolest woman on the planet, she told me to go. She and the Kiwi crowd will crash a party at someone's house in Earl's Court, like they do every year. One of the things I love about that woman is she doesn't know the meaning of passive aggressive. If Cass says, 'it's fine', then it's fine. If it isn't, she'll tell you straight. One time I wanted her to come with me to a lecture at Festival Hall on the Haida Gwaii, their culture and language. She said she'd enjoy that as much as I'd enjoy going to the Famous Three Kings pub to watch the Wallabies playing the Springboks. I got it. I attended the lecture on my own and wrote it up while she went to the pub for the rugby.

She does her thing, I do mine. And one of mine is the ex-uni crowd every other New Year's Eve. I suspect this time might well be the last.

In 2009 it was Simone's turn to organise, though it should have been Gael's. She missed out because of the reunion. She didn't complain. She never does. Part of me thinks Gael and I were twins separated at birth. If I was a woman, I'd wanna be Gael. She just gets it. You can tell her anything and she doesn't judge you. Cass thinks I'm secretly in love with her, but still says 'Go to Mallorca with your mates!' and doesn't get weird over it. I'm not in love with Gael, but I do love her. Kinda like a sister you'd protect and look out for and all. Though she's the last person who needs protecting.

Mallorca, Simone said. No way, we said. You're gonna be surprised, she said. No, knowing Simone, she probably said something like 'I think you will find yourselves surprised' because she went to finishing school. She was right. When I go somewhere fantastic, I tell people. Hey, man, I found this great bar, funky restaurant, cool island. You should check it out. I've never told anyone but Cass about Deià. No one but us and the residents should ever know about this magical, unspoilt, quirky corner of an island. Otherwise they'd all come and ruin it, then the poets and artists and dancers would leave for somewhere we don't know.

We rented a *finca*, a kind of ex-farmhouse with a pool and a path down to the sea. The beach wasn't private although to look at it you'd think so. The building was on a promontory with sea views from every window, and the sea spray crashing against the rocks was as hypnotic as a firework display. I loved it. As with everything I love, I wanted to share it with Cass, but she was in a pub in Kensington. That year, Simone brought a boyfriend – Jacques. He fitted in as if we'd known him for ten years. She should have stuck with that one. The nasty bastard she eventually married had millions, three houses and two teenage kids, but Jacques, man, Jacques could play the saxophone.

Boyfriends, wives, siblings, fine with me. But that year Gael invited her parents. We always said we could bring whoever we liked, but seriously, parents? Secretly, we all dreaded minding our manners with the older generation and privately muttered about her taking liberties. As it turned out, Kevin and Aoife were terrific company. Storytellers both, they had us all in stitches at every mealtime. They were interested in all of us and not afraid to ask direct questions. Aoife wanted to know if I was going to marry my girlfriend when I showed her a picture of Cass on my phone. When I told her I wasn't sure if I was ready to settle down, she laughed.

"Well, young fella, if what I hear is true, you must have a whole barn of wild oats if you've still more to sow."

Mika laughed so hard at that he actually cried.

The other thing that made it work was music. Kevin and Aoife were a well-honed double act who could make you laugh and weep. The local bar owner was also Irish, from Kerry, and pretty much claimed them as his own from the first night we walked in. Kevin played guitar, Aoife sang and Gael amazed us all with her skill on the bodhrán. Jacques joined in with his sax and the result was eclectic, bizarre and the best fun I'd had in years. We had the most entertaining New Year's Eve ever and I was ashamed of myself for ever thinking it should be our last.

Other people were the centre of attention and naturally I expected Simone to get mad and sulky. She didn't. She laughed, clapped and joined in as if she was happy. Who knows, maybe she was. By the pool, I wore my shades, pretending to read and watching the performance. She tinkled with laughter at some whispered comment from Jacques, trailed her fingers over his chest, sashayed past us to dive into the water, emerged wet and sleek, and with her wet bikini still clinging to her body, offered us more sangria.

I recognised these moves. She was out to seduce. But it wasn't Jacques and it certainly wasn't me. She had her sights set and locked on Mika. Poor bastard.

One day while we were still at university, I sat through my first morning lecture, absorbing no more information than the fact I was about to have a massive migraine. I walked home, closed the drapes and got into bed fully clothed. I guess I slept on and off for around three hours. When I awoke, that cotton-wool feeling was still there, but the pain had ceased. It was the middle of the day and Dhan and Simone wouldn't be home for hours yet. I shucked off my clothes and, treading with kittenish delicacy so as not to disturb my head, I shuffled my way to the kitchen for a glass of water.

The second I turned the corner, I could hear her voice. I stopped, not wanting to march in stark naked on Dhan and his girlfriend. But it couldn't be Dhan she was addressing as she was speaking French, fast and slangy. I understood the gist.

"What you don't understand is the background. He's funny, entertaining, the guy you're happy to introduce to your friends without embarrassment. He goes crazy for the French Maid routine and in bed, his enthusiasm makes up for a lack of technique. What I meant earlier was this. He is a practice run."

Another female voice, slightly lower in pitch. "What about the Canadian? I would give him a practice run."

"He's an American! He comes from Alaska and is not worth a second glance. A total *brânleur*. No wonder those two share a flat. Classic go-nowhere, do-nothing losers, with poor hygiene. Listen to me, *chouchou*, you and I deserve better."

The other girl mumbled something inaudible.

Simone laughed, with a hard, brassy tone I'd not noticed before. "Consider these days as the nursery slopes. We are refining our skills."

I retraced my steps into my bedroom, closed and locked the door. One word echoed around my head: '*brânleur*'. Roughly translated as wanker.

She was playing him. I had no idea how to break the news,

but Dhan had to know.

In the end, I did it with the help of Alanis Morissette. Two of the guys in our band had connections with the Montreux Jazz Festival. When I heard the rumour Morissette was headlining, I called in some favours and grabbed two tickets. *Jagged Little Pill* was a constant in our flat and seeing her perform live was the best birthday present I could give him. The plan was all set. At my suggestion, Gael and Lovisa would invite Simone to some kind of girls' night. Mika offered to chip in by paying for a decent hotel and I booked trains. On the night of Dhan's birthday, I'd spring the surprise on him and Simone. There was no way she could worm her way into that. *Les jeux sont faits.*

He was ecstatic. The double whammy was seeing Simone's nose way out of joint. She joined in the high-fives and congrats around the table, even if her exultations fell far below those of Mika and Lovisa.

Gael played it like a maestro. "Montreux? Oh, Dhan, what a bummer. You could always stay here if that Morissette female bores you to tears. Simone and I have plans to see *Merci la Vie* at Beaux Artes, eat seafood and slag off men. Can I tempt you?"

"You can tempt me!" said Lovisa, and the conversation fractured along gender lines.

Three weeks later, Dhan and I each packed an overnight bag and boarded the train to Montreux, full of excitement and well-armed for two days at a music festival. Clean underwear, change of shirt, two grams of cocaine, a bottle of tequila and some cold beers for the journey. Essential, as the train took well over an hour. We were reasonably well lubricated by the time we stepped off the CFF Interregio train, intent on two days of partying.

We dumped our bags at the hotel and hit the streets. Music was everywhere, with crowds milling from boulevard to lakeside garden to outdoor cafés. We people-watched from a terrace, grinning at first-timers fizzing with the novelty and old hands projecting sophistication, while we ate *Rösti* and drank more beer. Dhan told me about the gigs he'd seen in London, I shared my momentous events as a student in Montreal and we wandered through the throngs to get a view of the lake. Same lake we saw every day in Geneva, but an angle I hadn't tried before.

At the hotel, we took in the generosity of Mika's gesture. Two deluxe rooms in a four-star place with fruit bowls, a complimentary bottle of champagne and king-sized beds. That Czech champ, in his understated way, had pulled out all the stops. We showered, changed, drank the bubbles and snorted coke up to our eyeballs. Then, high as kites, we set off for the evening's entertainment. The atmosphere was fantastic, the weather balmy and we were right at the heart of it. I know because we kept telling each other the same thing.

The gig was at Miles Davis Hall and fewer than ten minutes' walk from our hotel. It took us over an hour to get there. I don't even recall what took so long, but we certainly stopped to refuel, more than twice. At least I had remembered the tickets.

My memories of the rest of the night are hazy. Dancing and singing along with Alanis, Dhan and me yelling 'She's amazing' about three hundred times, and clapping and cheering till my hands hurt. Afterwards, we stumbled around the streets and got chatting to a couple who'd been at the same concert. We had a few drinks with them and then decided to go back to the hotel and drink tequila on the balcony. I kept reminding myself to tell Dhan about Simone, but somehow the urgency had gone. Although both our rooms had balconies, Dhan had the better view, so we cracked open the bottle, raided the mini-bar for mixers and sat reliving the night while gazing at the view. We tried to be quiet, but kept getting excited. Finally the phone rang. It was the manager telling us in no uncertain terms on behalf of all the guests to get inside and close the door.

For some reason, we thought this was the funniest thing we'd ever heard. We shut the balcony windows and collapsed in a giggling heap on the bed. I poured us another drink and we sat up against the pillows, extolling the virtues of tequila and Coke. By then we were talking about the fizzy drink as we had long since run out of the powder. I found some Dutch courage and told Dhan what I had overheard. That seemed to sober him for a second. Then he said, "I don't give a fuck about Simone," and started laughing all over again. In my relief, I joined in and was soon helpless with laughter, tears rolling down my cheeks.

With no warning, Dhan leaned over and kissed me. I was taken aback, as I'd never got so much as a hint he was interested in men. My sexual preferences were no secret. If s/he's willing, count me in. I responded with an eagerness that scared me. I'd always had a thing for Dhan, so hid it well. We were flatmates, that's all. That night changed everything. It was getting light when all our passion was finally spent. We fell asleep in damp, tangled sheets. The last thing I remember before I passed out was Dhan telling me the story of how 'Smoke on the Water' was written in Montreux, as his hand stroked my chest hair.

When I woke up, my body was sending alarm signals from head, gut and bowels. Dhan's side of the bed was empty and I could hear him in the shower. With a groan of pain, I hauled my pounding head out of bed, dressed and went into my own room. It wasn't just the hangover, but that awful flat post-coke comedown. I swigged a bottle of sparkling water and had a long cool shower, wondering what the hell would happen next.

The phone rang as I was getting dressed.

"Hello?"

"Listen, mate, we need to check out. The cleaning staff have already knocked twice. We missed breakfast and should have been out of here an hour ago. You ready?" His tone was perfectly normal.

"Umm, yeah, almost."

"Good. See you downstairs in five. Let's get something to eat and then get a train home."

"You don't want to hang out here? Catch some more music?"

"I'm feeling a bit rough. I want to get home and sleep it off in my own bed."

"Right. See you downstairs."

He was waiting in the lobby and gave me a quick smile, but met my eyes for only a second. I checked out and we found a café on the way to the station. My stomach was roiling but we filled ourselves with carbs, while trying not to look at each other. It was painful. Eventually, I had to broach the subject.

"OK, so things can't get weird between ..."

He cut me off. "Hey, what happens in Montreux stays in Montreux, right? It was a one-off. Won't happen again."

His words cut deep and a realisation crept over me. The 'thing' I had for Dhan was more than just fancying him. I loved the guy. Last night might well have ruined our relationship, all because I couldn't resist the opportunity. Why was I so slow to understand my own feelings?

It was the worst time to have to face it, as physically, I felt like a bag of shit, but there was no other choice. "You're right. A one-off when we were both off our heads. Let's forget about it." As if.

Dhan wiped up the residue on his plate with a hunk of bread. "Yeah, let's. And, Clark? We never talk about it again. Not to each other or anyone else. No one can ever know, OK?" For the first time that morning, he looked into my eyes.

Why would I want to share the intimacy and tenderness of last night with anyone else? That was mine and mine alone.

"Know about what?" I forced a grin across my face. "Memory wiped and moving on. Are you going to finish those fries? Because I'm still hungry."

A crooked smile lifted his cheeks and something flashed in his eyes. Something I'd not seen before. "Have them. The amount you eat, you should be twice your size. How come I swim every other day, eat vegetarian food and still put on weight? Whereas you do virtually no exercise, eat all kinds of crap and don't carry an ounce of fat."

"Fast metabolism, mate," I said, helping myself to his leftovers. "By the time we get back to Geneva, I'll be hungry again. In fact, I might drop in on Mika and Lovisa to say thanks for helping me organise this weekend. And also to assist them with anything going from Sunday lunch."

He was watching me, his eyes soft. "It was a brilliant birthday present. Thank you. I had an unforgettable time."

I met his gaze. "So did I."

And that was a good place to leave it. "I need a piss. Will you ask the waitress for the bill?"

I kept my promise and told no one what happened that night. I'd have probably stayed silent till the grave if it wasn't for Gael. That woman has an instinct for what goes unsaid. She watched us, spotted the change in dynamic and asked me upfront if her theory was correct. All I did was confirm the truth. It was OK. You could trust Gael to keep a secret.

Chapter 9: Gael, now

Christmas with my family in 2019 was the worst yet. I think if the weather had been better, and we could have got out more, the stifling tension would have lessened. Southwold is a beautiful part of the world, with a fantastic coastline that stretches for miles. Perfect for walking off Christmas pudding. Yet three days of relentless rain, sly point-scoring from my brother and sister, hours of dreary television interrupted by huge, heavy meals, and I was crawling the walls.

My insufferable brother, who grew more pompous every year, had been banned from mentioning the current political situation for fear he and my sister would actually come to blows. Orla and I were of the same mind regarding the depressing mess, it's just she was ten times more passionate on the subject. Not surprising, I suppose, as she had to live with the consequences. But Brian held the diametrically opposite view and took every opportunity to justify his reasoning. Worse still, his vacuous wife with no opinions of her own agreed with everything he said.

Fed up to the back teeth with their offspring's squabbling, my parents warned us all that one more mention of politics and we would be asked to leave. That suited me fine. As an Irish journalist working in Brussels, I too had become weary of the debate.

We weren't due at the chalet in the Alps until Monday, but on

Boxing Day morning, I called Lovisa to see if I could spend the weekend with her in Geneva. Anything to get away from my family. She agreed immediately as she had spent Christmas alone.

"Can you come tomorrow?" she asked. "We could go to Harry's Bar and get plastered on cocktails. Just like the good old days."

Only Lovisa still uses expressions like 'plastered'. A sixty-year old in a forty-something's body. Simply hearing her voice cheered me up. "Definitely. If I can't get a flight, I'll take the train. I have to get out of here or there is a serious risk of my committing fratricide."

When I got out of the plane at Geneva airport, the sun was shining, the sky was blue and my spirits lifted like bubbles. Three days of hanging out with an old mate in our university city would repair all the damage wrought by my blood(y) relatives. Lovisa's apartment was a decent size and in a nice part of town. Knowing the price of rents in Geneva, I was surprised she could afford it on her NGO salary. I asked no questions, just grateful that she had a spare room.

She seemed delighted to see me and laughed at my horror stories of a family Christmas. Her skin was golden and her figure trim. I told her she looked great.

"Thank you. I only got back from Ghana on the twentieth. The tan hasn't faded yet."

"What were you doing in Ghana? The teenage mother stuff again?" I asked.

"Not this time. A team of us were training nurses and midwives. It was a lot more optimistic than my usual gigs. You know, Ghana is such a beautiful place. I was thinking, maybe the next time we celebrate New Year's together, we should go somewhere other than Europe."

"We don't always go to Europe," I protested. "We've been to

New York."

"Once," said Lovisa. "In twenty years, we've only ever visited one other continent."

I calculated. "I guess you're right. Maybe it's because I've travelled so much and visited so many places, that meeting up with you lot in a European city feels like my second home."

"Talking of second homes, let's get down to Harry's Bar. There are a couple of mojitos with our names on them."

On Saturday, we took a train to Lausanne and wandered along the lake in a biting wind. We sent Simone a message to see if she wanted to join us but there was no reply. Lovisa seemed withdrawn and far less chatty than she had been the night before. I put it down to a hangover and didn't worry too much as I was enjoying the sight of Lac Leman. That view never got tired. When the cold started to hurt, we took refuge in a lakeside café and ordered *cafés crèmes*.

"I still cannot believe it will be twenty years," said Lovisa, her gaze on the mountains across the water.

Of all of us, Lovisa was the one who wanted to talk about it the most.

"I know. Weird how it turned out that the first time I got to organise was the twentieth anniversary." I paused, thinking back to 2009 in Mallorca, one of the happiest reunions we'd had. "Twenty years. Sometimes it's like a bad dream."

She looked at me, her eyes the colour of the bottle of Bombay Sapphire. "I've been seeing a counsellor again. First time in fifteen years I felt the need."

"Because of the anniversary?" I asked.

She shrugged and took a sip of coffee. "The question is, which anniversary? I know, I know. You're talking about Dhan's death. Me too. I'm also talking about the death of my relationship, the death of Simone's unborn child, the death of all our innocences. 2000 was the most horrible year of my life. I honestly believe that if we hadn't had each other and I hadn't found a counsellor, I wouldn't have made it this far."

There was no answer to that. Against my will, my mind went back to those wretchedly miserable months. The police investigation, that nightmarish meeting with Dhan's family, the inquest, Mika and Lovisa splitting up, Simone aborting Dhan's baby, Mika's attempt on his own life and the tears, all those tears. I drank my coffee and shook my head, as if that could release me from the chain to the past.

"Is it the same counsellor?" I asked. It was a banal question but I could think of nothing else to say. The real question I didn't dare ask.

Lovisa shook her head. "No, this is a new one. Her angle is progress rather than forgiveness. It's a long time since I forgave all of us for the part we played. Mika, Simone, Clark, me and even Dhan. Everyone except you."

I snapped my head up to face her. "Except me? Why do I get off scot-free?"

She reached across the table and pushed a lock of hair off my forehead. "Because, Gael, you weren't there."

Maybe it was the maternal gesture or the beatific tone, but a surge of anger boiled up in me and I had to get away from her or release something vicious. I approached the counter to ask the waitress where to find the bathroom. Once locked into a shiny tiled cubicle, I sat on the seat and breathed.

Always the same. It wasn't Gael's fault. Gael wasn't there. Gael has no reason to feel guilty. It's worse for us. We were present at the moment of our friend's death. She wasn't there. I breathed and breathed until my jaw began to relax. Finally, I unlocked the cubicle and washed my face and hands. Only then did I return to the café.

Lovisa was wearing her other favourite expression: worried. "Gael, I'm sorry, did I upset you? That wasn't my intention."

I drank my coffee, cooler now. "No, you didn't. Just … maybe some of this stuff should stay between you and your counsellor. You know what I mean?"

We paid for our coffees and walked back to the train station without a word.

That evening, I suggested watching a film. We ordered pizza, got into our pyjamas and sat side by side on the sofa laughing at a chick lit comedy. After it was over, Lovisa emptied the dregs of the wine bottle into our glasses and switched off the TV set. We chatted idly about underrated female comedians and picked at pizza crusts. Simone messaged to say she was skiing with her sister and would go directly to the chalet. She sent us both love and a picture of herself on the slopes.

As always, her beauty dazzled. She still looked in her late twenties despite the fact all of us had turned forty in the past couple of years. When we first met, her head-turning loveliness caused me pain. Like Mika's wealth, Simone's looks seemed to give her an unfair advantage in the world, and I used to resent that. Not anymore. Since Dhan's death, I'd given up envy.

"That girl could wear a sack and make it look desirable," said Lovisa. "She doesn't seem to age at all. I got a picture somewhere from that time we were in Kefalonia. When was that? 2003?" She hopped up and opened a cupboard.

"No, Clark took us to Berlin in 2003, remember? Kefalonia must have been 2005. Simone organised that one. I think of all our reunions, and I know we're not allowed to have favourites, but I liked the islands best." My eyes were drooping and I was ready for bed.

"Here it is! Kefalonia *was* 2005. We're getting forgetful in our old age." Lovisa flopped onto the sofa beside me with a photograph album. Actual photographs stuck behind clear film, each labelled and captioned in Lovisa's neat handwriting. The woman was an anachronism and I loved her for it.

We huddled together and pored over the pictures,

reminiscing and reminding each other of details one of us had forgotten. There was Simone, standing on a beach in Old Skala with a hand to her eyes, shielding her face from the sun. We compared it to the picture we had recently received. Lovisa was right. Simone had hardly aged at all.

It must have been the wine, warmth and tiredness, but in so many of the group pictures, I saw five friends and one shadow. A space where there should have been a man. There were some shots of the last evening, too. I was missing in most, because I was taking them. One group shot with automatic release showed the six of us at the dinner table in that small room. I could almost taste the burnt soup, smell the beer cheese and feel the warmth of the fire, friendship and that bloody uncomfortable dress. Something was wrong in that picture, but I couldn't put my finger on it. That nagging doubt surfaced again. Like there was something obvious that had been there all these years. I was just too close to see it.

When we turned the final page, folded brown papers dropped into my lap like autumn leaves. One fell to the floor. I picked it up, unfolded it and recognised a grease-spotted place mat from 1999. This one was Clark's and it bore a quotation from F. Scott Fitzgerald's *The Great Gatsby*, inspirational messages from each of us and twenty-year-old stains of fish soup and red wine. Even in the awful aftermath of the accident, she had kept our mementoes safe. I opened one after another, reading Lovisa's neat script, my own drunken scrawl and the distinctive handwriting of Simone, Clark, Mika and, oh sweet Lord, Dhan.

In a second, I was there, then, full of bullish optimism for every one of us, scrawling confident words of love and hope and because I couldn't help myself, an in-joke. My nose prickled, and tears I thought long dried made a triumphant comeback. I cried for them, those six young idiots who thought the new millennium was all theirs.

Lovisa closed the album and we sat in silence, staring at the flames in the fake fire. Neither of us seemed to have the energy to move.

"Gael? I want to apologise for earlier. I've been thinking about it and I realise that saying I didn't need to forgive you because you weren't there takes away your grief, in a way. That's unfair and minimises your feelings while claiming both grief and guilt for myself. I'm sorry for my selfish thinking."

I blew my nose on a pizza napkin. "It's fine. It really is." It really was. I was over it and could do without second-hand therapy speak.

"Thank you for saying that. I'm embarrassed about how badly I expressed myself. You see, my intention was meant to be the opposite of patronising. What I wanted to say this morning was a kind of confession."

I couldn't take any more revelations about the past. I hauled myself upright, feeling the effects of the wine. "I need to sleep on this." I bent to kiss her on both cheeks. "Goodnight, sleep tight, and thank you for keeping our memories safe. See you in the morning."

Her smile was kind as I left her, staring into artificial flames.

As for me, I lay awake in the spare room, eyes puffy and throat sore. My emotional brain murmured reassuring mantras and advised sleep. My journalist brain added these latest pieces of evidence to the file labelled 'Was It Really An Accident?' A file I would likely never close.

"Because, Gael, you weren't there."

Chapter 10: Mika, 2011

To my mind, we had become far too smug and Eurocentric. I'm the first one to say it's important to be proud of your home country, your home continent and admire all it has achieved. Nevertheless, that should not be to the detriment of other countries, continents, places with something different to offer. A cultural openness allows us to learn from other ways of doing things and prevents us from becoming set in our ways, moving from patriotism to nationalism. We are not always right.

Listen to me, proselytising. I used to talk like that a lot, in speeches rather than conversation, especially when Lovisa and I were a couple. We fell into that self-satisfied trap of thinking we were always right. Because we agreed on politics, religion, and lifestyle – *mens sana in corpore sano* – the two of us thought we knew best. We judged our friends. If I'm honest, we judged everyone. Since then, I've changed. Lovisa, not so much. I still see judgement in her eyes and those moments make me think it's probably best we split up. Together, we'd have become insufferable.

Just to shake things up a bit, I suggested New York. More than suggested, if I'm honest. I presented the opportunity much like I had presented the chance to jump on a frozen lake. An experience we could all benefit from. Look how that turned out.

No, this was not the same thing at all. New York City on New

Year's Eve had everything to offer. I fixed us an apartment in Harlem, I booked tickets to a show, I researched restaurants and festive events we could attend to make the most out of a few days in the city that never sleeps. To my astonishment, everyone went for it.

Lovisa was the most enthusiastic. She had already mentioned several times we should go further afield for our celebrations. However, her rationale was mainly for the sun, and we wouldn't be getting much of that in New York. I managed to get her on side by mentioning iconic locations we knew from the movies: Grand Central Station, the Empire State building, Brooklyn Bridge, Central Park, the New York Public Library, Times Square and Fifth Avenue. In the kind of way that I can understand, Clark was the least enthusiastic. The man was a totally committed Europhile and had no interest in returning to the United States. But even he, having never been to the city, agreed it would be fun to go somewhere completely new and play tourists.

I had a secondary reason for going to America – language. As linguists, there was always an undercurrent of competition between us. It was never overt, but whenever we were in another country, Germany, Greece, France, Spain, one of us always spoke the language better than the rest. Gael had spent a year living in Munich, so naturally took the lead in Berlin (although Simone tried her best to compete). Lovisa's Greek eased us through Kefalonia, Simone's French took charge in Geneva or Corsica, and in his laid-back way Clark was our go-to man in Majorca.

My languages – Czech, Russian, French and English – put me at a disadvantage. We would never return to the Czech Republic, obviously. And the likelihood of us spending on New Year in Moscow or St Petersburg was remote. My one advantage was working with American developers on my new business. I had spent many months in Silicon Valley, hiring the right kind of technicians to realise my translation app. I understood America.

Whether in San Francisco, New York, or Houston, I was comfortable. That was why I selected the Big Apple as a level playing field.

Everyone had a great time. We adopted our tourist personae with enthusiasm. Nothing was too tacky, cheap or obvious because this was a once-in-a-lifetime experience. We took the ferry to Staten Island. We rode the elevator to the top of the Empire State building. We flew around Manhattan in a helicopter. We travelled back and forth to Harlem on the subway or in yellow taxis, exclaiming at the novelty of feeling like we were in a movie. We ate Cajun food in a basement, pancakes in a diner, hot dogs on the street and had a five-course meal in the meatpacking district on New Year's Eve. Everything was exactly as it should have been and although we are not supposed to claim any of these events as personal victories, I think everyone would agree that was one of the best reunions we have ever had.

On New Year's Day, Simone and Lovisa were up early, ready to hit the sales. The thought of fighting my way through aggressive crowds to grab a bargain sounded hellish, so I bailed out. Gael was still in bed, but Clark offered to go as far as downtown with them, before making his way to Ground Zero. A friend of his had lost his life there in 9/11 and he wanted to pay his respects. It wasn't the kind of thing where you could tag along. They left and I opened my laptop to answer a few emails. When Gael got up, we talked each other into taking the subway to Central Park. We wanted to use the opportunity to eat a Danish without Simone screaming blue murder about the concept of putting cheese on a pastry.

January 1, 2012 was freezing. Gael and I emerged from Columbus Circle station into a crisp frosty day. I pulled my hat down over my ears and Gael tucked her gloved hand into the crook of my arm. We walked along the paths, taking photographs, admiring the scenery, greeting mounted police officers and soaking in the atmosphere of a brand new year. As we passed the horse and cart taxi rank, we briefly considered giving one of the ponies some exercise until Gael pointed out that after last night, we needed it more. It didn't take long before the charm of frosty branches and blue sky wore off and the sense of frozen feet and cold faces drove us out of the park and into a café. We sat at a window, idly watching passers-by, drinking chocamocha something and eating a blue cheese Danish.

We were sniggering together at some fashion victim making his or her way up the street in ridiculous boots when Gael asked a question. "Are you pissed off with us, after last night?"

Truthfully, it was worse than that. I was infuriated at the short-sighted attitudes of my university friends and personally disappointed that they could not appreciate the generosity of my gesture. I was trying to make things right.

"No. Of course not. Everyone is entitled to refuse a gift and the giver should not take that to heart. I'm not pissed off with any of you although I do think you will regret your decision."

She nodded, continuing to eat her pastry with a knife and fork. "I can't speak for the others, only for myself. So thank you for offering us the opportunity to invest in your company. It's been on my mind all morning. My decision remains the same as do my reasons for saying no. My primary concern is not having sufficient funds but my second is a golden rule. I never mix friendship and business. It's got nothing to do with trust, as I know you are a brilliant business person. I just don't want a financial bond tangled up with our emotional connection."

I laughed, shaking my head. In effect, Gael was handing me a microphone and it was time to come clean to the cameras.

"Right, I want to tell you something. If you think it's important enough, you can share it with the others. All I will say is this, I don't think it's anyone else's business."

"Mika, I'm not a journo today. I'm your friend and you don't owe me any kind of explanation. Plus I've got a hangover. My head isn't up for any major shit. I can just about cope with ordering another coffee." She signalled to the barista for two refills.

"I'm telling you because you are my friend. You stuck by me when I was at my worst. In 2000, most people thought I'd lost it, obsessing about finding his corpse. In a way, I suppose I had lost my sense of perspective. My unrelenting drive to find Dhan was not to see the body and accept he was dead. It was because I couldn't let him get away with it."

The barista arrived with two more mugs of chocolate-coffee marshmallow stuff and Gael sighed. Whether that was the prospect of the coffee or my outpourings, I don't know.

She licked a spoon and rested her face on her hand. "Come on, spit it out."

"OK. I first heard about this translation concept in 1997. While we were at college, the idea of artificial intelligence and translation was in its infancy. But some people had taken the first steps from theory to practice. A friend told me about this start-up and I was curious. On top of that, it was obvious to everyone I had seed capital. One of our professors even put his name to the proposal. It will come as no surprise to you that the person who brokered the deal was Dhan. The business plan was brilliant, the costings seemed accurate and the financial backing was largely in place. I gave Dhan thirty grand as one of four stakeholders in the project."

"That is amazing! So your business now was originally conceived by Dhan. He'd be so stoked to see the success you've made of it."

I shook my head, my eyes closed.

"What? Mika, what is it?"

"That is not the case, Gael. After Dhan's death, I was a mess, as you probably remember. Once back on my feet and through my final exams, I contacted the company to check up on progress. It was the first time I had made personal contact due to the fact all previous dealings had gone through Dhan."

Gael put down her mug. She clearly knew or guessed what was coming next.

"The project had run out of steam in the early part of 1999. Dhan 'invested' my money in a project that was already failing and collapsed three months later."

"Mika!" Gael's voice was a whisper.

I opened my eyes. "I know. What is thirty grand to a rich Czech kid? Chicken feed, right? Wrong. That was my trust fund. Trust, ha! My parents trusted me to use it wisely. And I threw it all away on an ambitious idea. It took me years to recover from that, mentally and financially. When the dust settled, I went back to the idea and with cold, clear eyes; I acknowledged my initial response was correct. It was a good concept. Not the kind of idea a bunch of twenty-year-olds could knock out in a couple of months, but something a team of carefully sourced experts might be able to develop in a matter of years. Which is exactly what I did. I got my 30K back, Gael, and more besides. Yeah, you should invest. We're going to have a very happy set of shareholders."

"I'm sure you will. But I won't be one of them. You mean more to me than a cash cow." She picked up her coffee and hesitated. "When did you invest that money?"

"June 17, 1998. I have the contracts, not that they're worth anything other than a lesson."

She studied me. "Over a year and a half later, you still didn't know the company had gone under? That's not like you, Mika. You dot all the Is and cross all the Ts. You're telling me you never even checked?"

The sun was setting and I sat back into the shadow. Maybe this was why I wanted to tell her. Gael had an infallible instinct for picking up on detail. "I couldn't check. I trusted Dhan to inform me on progress. He delivered regular reports and I had every reason to feel optimistic. Except my gut told me something was not quite right. My plan was to ask for an update on New Year's Day. I would suggest a walk in the forest, during which Dhan and I would fall behind. I knew exactly the right detour. When I was convinced the two of us were alone, I would pin him down and grill him for some answers. But that never happened. Because the night before that conversation, he jumped into the lake and disappeared. Like a fish off the hook."

Chapter 11: Gael, now

On Sunday morning, when I got up there was a note from Lovisa on the kitchen table beside the pizza boxes.

Good morning! I hope you slept well. I had a call from the office first thing. There's been a break-in. Bloody buggers! As the boss, I need to get down there and make a statement to the police. No idea as to damage or losses till I see it for myself. Who the damned hell would rob a charity over Christmas? Help yourself to breakfast and I'll call around lunchtime. Mika's flight gets in at two, so if I'm not back by then, can you let him in? Lx

Lovisa's swearing was even milder than my mother's. I made myself French toast and coffee, and browsed the newspapers till eleven, then decided to hit the supermarket to forage provisions for our chalet holiday. Lovisa called my mobile while I was at the checkout. She was going to be there for another couple of hours, so I assured her I would welcome Mika. It occurred to me to vacate the spare room. After all, Mika had made the request before me. Then I thought about the fuss he would make, insisting I take the bed while he slept on the sofa. It wasn't worth it.

Something propelled me to the cupboard and the photo album we had pored over last night. I flicked through to the group shot which bugged me so much. Again, something stung. As if certain elements in the picture didn't belong there ...

somehow the balance was off. I went through every detail on the table, all the cards and symbols, dishes and glasses. The wall behind us. The clothes we were wearing. Our young faces smiling. Then I noticed Dhan's body language.

It signalled the complete opposite of his smiling face. At first I thought his tense hunch was because he'd hurried back from the timer, but he hadn't. Only I came rushing back from the camera, giggling under the time pressure. There I was, smile broad, eyes wide, with a hideous haircut.

I put my thumb over Dhan's head, focusing only on his posture. He was bunched like a sprinter, shoulders stiffened, his torso slightly angled away from the group. It might have been the split second of the shot, yet his face showed the perfect photo session cheese. His body spoke a different language. It was full of fear. He wanted to escape.

On a whim, I decided to meet Mika at the airport. The gesture was born mostly out of eagerness to see him and just a little from a desire to have some one-to-one conversation before Lovisa returned. I waited by the barriers in Arrivals scrutinising each wave of travellers as they came through the double doors. Finally a long, rangy figure emerged wearing a puffa jacket and a beanie hat. He wasn't expecting anyone to meet him and strode off in the direction of the trains. I hurried in his wake and caught his arm.

"Gael! What are you doing here? This is a lovely surprise!" He kissed me on both cheeks and hugged me tight.

"I'm your welcoming committee. Did you have a nice flight, sir, can I take your bag, sir, I'm afraid the limo's in the shop, sir, so we have to take the train."

"That limo is very unreliable. Do you know, I cannot remember a single occasion when I've arrived in Geneva and it has been functional? I blame the driver."

"Me too. You look great! Healthy as a hound. Are you still

running?" I sped up to keep pace with his long strides.

"Of course. I'm planning to do a triathlon in the spring. What's the news with you? And where are Lovisa and Simone?"

He stood to face me as we travelled below ground on the escalator. With him two steps below me, our heads were almost level.

"I'm fine, other than a shitty Christmas. Family, don't ask. Lovisa is fine other than a shitty break-in at her office. That's where she is right now talking to the police. Simone will meet us at the chalet. She's skiing with one of her sisters." A thought occurred to me. "Are you lot going to be all winter sports and healthy living this week? I'm not sure I can stand that."

The train pulled in. We found a couple of seats and Mika lifted his suitcase up onto the overhead ledge with as much ease as if it were a bar of chocolate. He sat opposite me, his slate-coloured eyes crinkling into a smile.

"Good heavens, no. Apart from the snowboarding, cross-country skiing, mountain hikes and rock climbing, it's going to be beer and cakes all the way." He reached forward and squeezed my knee. "You're going to love the après ski. How is Brussels?"

I shrugged. "I'm sure you read the news. The needle has been stuck in the same groove for the past four years. As a journalist, trying to write something new about the situation is like trying to hatch stones. How is Bratislava?"

Mika got to his feet to help a woman in a burqa stow her case. She thanked him in French and took her child to sit at the table opposite.

"Bratislava? Right now, it's minus 16° and dark. Not that I notice because work is incredibly exciting. The translation app is now in its third iteration and more popular than ever. All those years of research finally bear fruit. And when I say fruit, I'm talking watermelons."

I laughed. "I assume that's Mika-speak for massively successful. Or in Gael-speak, you're earning a wad thick enough to choke a donkey."

His laughter was infectious. The Muslim lady and her child reacted with shy smiles and two older ladies gave him an appreciative once-over.

"As always, Gael-speak wins again. Yes, in Slovakian terms, my salary is exceptional. It probably equates to a Swiss supermarket worker by now."

From the train we boarded a tram and arrived at Lovisa's place just shy of four o'clock. Of our hostess, there was no sign. Mika and I went through the motions of arguing about which of us should have the spare room and he placed his suitcase behind the sofa. I made a rough snack of cheese, cold meats and bread with a bottle of cheap table wine from my morning's shop. We sat at the table, grazing, chatting and recalibrating. I hadn't seen this man for two years and every time I did so, I remembered how much I liked the guy.

"… because the thing that most translation systems lack is nuance. It's genuinely impossible to provide an accurate translation service without cultural context. I know, I know, I'm preaching to the converted. But once we did that by taking phrases which when translated literally have no logic and put them within a cultural context, the meaning changes. That's what makes this far more sophisticated than any other language translation program available. We are currently only at the European level although our investors can see what a crucial resource we've created. This is going global, my friend."

"Long may you reign!" I said, raising my glass. "Makes me wish I'd invested now. You did give us all the chance."

Mika's face clouded and he sat back in his chair. I waited, nibbling on a piece of brie, until he was ready to speak.

"Gael, I offered you and all the others the opportunity to invest because this was not my idea. It's not new or original; it's just that I took it as far as I could go and with the help of some brilliant IT experts and extraordinary translators, took it that bit further. What you need to understand is that…"

My phone buzzed. A message from Lovisa. `Leaving now, home by six. Lx.`

I looked up at Mika. "She's on her way. But you were in the middle of something. About the translation app." I kept my voice light. "I wanted to ask you about that, actually. Last year, I met Professor Leigh when he was in Brussels to address the EU on the subject of research funding. He agreed to an interview. I thought he might give me some insider titbits, but it was actually dull as ditch water. I mentioned your translation app to him and he remembered putting his name to the original idea. The funny thing was…"

Mika froze. "The funny thing was?"

I folded my arms and looked him in the eye.

He stared back at me, his jaw set to stubborn. Then he laughed. "I should have known. I guess, deep down, that's why I told you. Because you of all people would not let go. The funny thing was … the project collapsed from lack of funding. So you put two and two together and worked out that my investment never reached them. Am I right?"

I nodded. "Which leads me to believe Dhan scammed you out of thirty grand. Am I right?"

He took several seconds to reply, scratching his stubble. "Yes, I'm ashamed to admit that's exactly what happened. For a long time, I didn't accept it myself. It was more than just the money, it was the betrayal. I still don't know how he thought he would get away with it. I have no idea what he did with the money and under the circumstances, there was absolutely no chance of my asking his family to give it back." He shook his head, his gaze distant, then brought his focus back to me. "Did you really meet the professor or did you just go digging?"

I shrugged and gave him a guilty grin. I had to keep him onside because I had one more vital question. "A bit of both. I did meet him in Brussels, but his memory was not great. I had to follow up with a few phone calls. Mika, when did you find out?"

There was a long silence as the room grew darker around us. Eventually, we heard a door slam somewhere in the building. Lovisa must be home.

I looked up and met Mika's eyes, shadowed as they were in the dusky light.

His voice, when it came, was little more than a whisper. "The day before we broke up for Christmas. I went round to their apartment with every intention of beating the shit out of that devious bastard. But of course, he'd already left. What I said to you before was true. My plan was to challenge him on New Year's Day. But what I had in store was a bit more than some probing questions. I wanted revenge."

The sound of Lovisa's key in the lock interrupted him.

He caught my hand. "The fact remains, Gael, he still got away with it." He stood up as the door opened. "Lovisa! It's great to see you!"

"Hi, Mika! Why the dickens are you two sitting in the dark?"

Chapter 12: Lovisa, 2013

When it came around to my turn to organise the reunion again, I cheated a little. The latter part of the year I spent in the Democratic Republic of Congo working with teenage mothers, so the idea of arranging a party for my university friends was not high on my priority list. Somehow it seemed obscene to weigh up villas or apartments with ensuite bathrooms while young rape victims were trying to comprehend the extra layer of responsibility involved with unexpected parenthood. It was early December when it occurred to me I had to act fast or fail the others.

So I cheated. I called a colleague in Geneva who worked for the same NGO. Her mother had a family home on Corsica she would let to trusted tenants. By some miracle, it wasn't yet booked and I got it for a stupidly cheap rate. No discussion, I sent the group the details, dates and share of the cost and said take it or leave it. They took it. Best of all, it was another island.

One of the happiest get-togethers was in Deià, Mallorca in 2009. It should have been one of the saddest, since it was the ten-year anniversary, but that island put a spell on us. I keep saying I'll return one day, but I know I won't. Things wouldn't be the same. Corsica was as close as I could get to recreating the joy of Deià.

It was also the year I fell in love for the first time since Mika.

I'd resigned myself to being single after I'd met and lost my soul mate. Sex was still something I craved occasionally, rather like a Chinese takeaway, and it was almost as easy to find. Love was not. Mainly because I consigned the very idea to a box in the cellar labelled Things I'll Never See Again. I wish I could add one other thing to that box – the image of his face when I told him what Simone and I had done. Unfortunately, that is burnt onto my mind and can never be removed.

On the day I arrived at training camp in Kinshasa, I saw a face I trusted immediately. His name was Fabrice; he was Congolese and a guide for the doctors, nurses and translators working for Médecins Sans Frontières. People say the eyes are the windows to the soul. Fabrice's eyes were full-length French windows with a view of campfires, music and the kind of sunsets only seen in Africa. His tiny kindnesses, polite demeanour and sense of control endeared us all to this lean, rangy man. Yet it was his loss of control, the fire within, that drew this moth to the flame.

On NGO aid missions, after the day's work is done, there is a whole lot of sex. It's not about lust, but comfort. Everyone seeks a warm place, some skin-to-skin solace, a place of safety and a (generally) willing partner. Abuses occur, I don't deny that, and it's another layer of self-policing we must undertake. Overall, quiet intimacies under canvas are not about physical gratification, more a craving for tenderness and security, moments where we can heal from the draining days. I've taken those moments where I can get them and feel no shame. You give as much as you get.

Fabrice was no comfort blanket. Parts of me began buzzing each time I saw him and only some of them were due to physical urges. Despite all this man had witnessed, he had a compassionate mind and an optimistic view of the future. That, coupled with an intelligent analysis of how to achieve it, made him irresistibly attractive in my eyes. We stayed up late by the fire, talking in low voices about social change and improving our world. Or we'd get up early, fetch water and spend an hour crushing *pondu* leaves together to make at least one nutritious meal of the day for our young mothers. Fabrice nourished me.

On one of the trips to Kinshasa, a gruelling five-hour ride in a geriatric Jeep, Fabrice and I were alone. It was risky to stop, even more so after we'd picked up the miserable selection of medicines we could afford, because of bandits, thieves and kidnappers. We asked for refuge overnight within the walled compound of a mission, accepted a bowl of rice each and slept in the vehicle. My bones creaked, my muscles ached and sweat crusted my skin. That night, we lay in each other's arms, touching, kissing, holding, caressing and releasing. It was nothing like my conventional idea of love-making, but his touch was so gentle and tender, I surrendered.

At dawn, the monsoon pounded on the roof of the Jeep like war drums. We disentangled ourselves and wriggled outside, washing off the sticky sweat and stealing a natural power shower in the deluge of the rains. Never in my life had I been so abandoned and so alive.

Back at camp, he sneaked into my tent almost every night, unless he was on night watch. We held each other, kissed each other and made love for so long we were exhausted. His one rule was no penetration. We had no condoms and the threat of STDs was constant – we spent most days teaching people how to avoid spreading infection. I once joked we should video ourselves practising what we preached and share it with our students. His body stiffened and he retreated into silence. I never mentioned it again.

I loved him! I loved him so much it was a constant fire, a burning in my stomach, my heart, my groin. Even while administering vaccines or demonstrating how to bottle feed, my fingers were dissatisfied. All they wanted was his skin. My mind worried away at the knotty problem of how to bring him with me to New Year's Eve. He had a passport but no visa. Getting a flight at this late notice was all but impossible. How would my friends react? His French was perfect, so we could all converse, but what would they think? Who cared what they thought! The crucial question was, how would he react? The committed volunteer, dedicated to supporting developing countries, takes her week off to fly herself and exotic boyfriend to a European island, drink wine, play facile games and eat enough to feed this compound for a year. I couldn't expose myself to that kind of judgement.

He took me to the airport, told me not to worry and kissed me goodbye. Tears ran down my face the entire flight and I blew my nose so much so the man next to me moved to another seat. He probably thought I had a cold or something worse.

While waiting for the bus, I gave myself a stern talking-to. *You get to spend a week in a rich country, with hot and cold running water, a full fridge, a soft bed with clean sheets, good company and nothing at all to worry about. How dare you spoil it all by feeling guilty and missing the man you left behind? Enjoy this week, take advantage of every single privilege, restore yourself and take all that goodness back with you to him, to them.*

It always took us a day to acclimatise. So much had changed. Simone newly married, Clark freshly divorced, Mika fired up by his business (and romantic) partner and Gael always on the trail of a new story or love affair. I made up my mind not to share Fabrice. Our reunions were a safe space, but I understood it was sometimes better to hold on to your secrets. The threads binding Fabrice and me were so delicate and fragile, yet the strongest bond I had ever known. Apart from Mika.

I would never confess this to anyone, not even my best friends, but I had never really got over losing the love of my life. Mika and I were destined for one another. The horrific nightmare of Dhan's death and Simone's termination on top of our own emotional vulnerability ruined our chances in the early days. Even so, I believed we would get another opportunity. People use the expression 'soul mate' far too easily. The truth is, when you meet yours, you know it. Circumstances may keep you apart, but there is a part of you, deeper than heart, deeper than sensibility, just raw instinct that tells you, this is it. This is the missing jigsaw piece you've been seeking. For me, that was Mika.

I loved him. I wanted him to be happy. If he wasn't with me, that was sad, but better than trying to force him into something he didn't want. My counsellor suggests my motivation for arranging the New Year's Eve reunions was to maintain that contact, keep the door open, no matter how much I suffered by seeing him with other women. I think she's oversimplifying.

There were eight of us in 2013. The usual five, plus Simone's husband, Mika's partner and Clark's best friend. We worked really hard, being inclusive, upbeat, exploratory and enthusiastic, but the week was a total washout. Clark, his mate and Simone's husband got themselves locked into some kind of macho competition which caused constant aggression in everything we did. Mika refused to take part, shrugging off their drinking games, athletics and argumentative debates as sexual frustration. This did nothing to endear him to any of us. Instead, he turned inwards, canoodling with his lovely Slovakian girlfriend. I don't even remember her name, only her eyebrows.

Gael and I could not absent ourselves from the dynamic as we had to support Simone. We walked the glorious countryside, enjoyed the food and found some moments, some pockets of peace. I ate fresh vegetables, showered every day and even got a haircut from Mika's girlfriend. She did a good job. For me there were practical advantages but the usual emotional shot in the arm was absent. When I said goodbye, I wondered if we would, if we should ever do this again. These people were my closest friends. Imagining life without them made me tearful.

Though nothing like the tears that assaulted me when I found my visa to return to the Democratic Republic of Congo had been revoked. I could not go back. I spent ten days in a hostel in Marseille, making a daily trek back and forth to the consulate, pleading my case. I couldn't communicate with Fabrice; no phones, no computers, not even a fax machine. Via the team in Geneva, I discovered our entire NGO had been thrown out of the country, leaving our compound, our patients, our supporters and our team on the ground abandoned. The UN agreed to listen to our appeal and attempt to negotiate on our behalf, which would take months if not years. Friends scrambled enough money to get me home to my flat, where I at least had the advantage of communication systems. It wasn't enough. The DRC had closed down and refused to let us return. All those young girls, all their babies, all those people trying to help. We could do nothing but leave them behind.

Eight months later, I received an electronic communication from the mission where we had once stayed. Father Ali told me how the refuge had been taken over by the militia. Thanks to previous warnings, he and other religious leaders had rescued many of the inhabitants and their offspring. The support network of nurses, security guards, drivers and guards had dispersed, left to their own devices. He didn't mention Fabrice.

Chapter 13: Gael, now

Winter sports are an insane idea and people who enjoy flinging themselves down mountains at breakneck speed are certifiable, in my opinion. Lovisa, Mika and Simone had grown up on skis or snowboards, plus Clark's Alaskan childhood gave him a lasting passion for the great outdoors. My idea of getting some exercise was a nice walk along a beach to a pub, ideally in late spring or early autumn. The type of weather that's not too hot, not too cold and perfect for having a pint of real ale in the pub garden. Switzerland even has a 'sports holiday' in the winter for families to rush off up alpine mountains, wear themselves out and eat fondue. Not for me, thanks. On this, Dhan and I had always agreed. In the winter, as Dhan used to say, activities should be all about The Great Indoors. He kept up his swimming regime all year round, in a nice heated pool with a hot tub outside. I joined him one winter while the others had gone skiing, just for the tub part. I could see the attraction of sitting in warm steamy water while snowflakes fell on our heads.

It seemed appropriate for the twentieth anniversary that we returned to Geneva. The city is a moody diva. Sometimes she steps onto the stage in full sparkling sunshine, peaks crisp, lake glittering and defies you not to fall in love with her forever. Other times, she's cold and sulky, refusing to perform, shrouding her finery in grey, wet clouds. Today, she was throwing spiteful sheets of sleet in our eyes and lashing our cheeks with razor-like winds. Mika, Lovisa and I took another trip to the Asian market to get another bunch of ingredients for our banquet, picked up the hire car and Mika drove us out of the city towards the mountains.

Once we ascended above the gloomy mists, the sun's reflection on the snowy landscape made us all reach for our sunglasses. Blue sky, snow-dusted forests and clear tarmac roads delineated by those red poles to guide the snow-ploughs signalled we were in mountain territory. We should be over it by now. Switzerland is pretty, we know that better than most. But it can still take my breath away. Spirits raised and anticipation high, we drove through jaw-dropping terrain, snapping pictures of towering glaciers and shadowed valleys. Mika drove past charming villages with shuttered windows and *colombage* walls, thinning out as we drove the final kilometres to our chalet. Tension rose up my spine and into my shoulders. *It's too far from any shops. It's cut off from civilisation. If it's shit, everyone will blame me. Why did I choose something so ridiculously remote?*

When we eventually crested the snowy driveway, the chalet was lit up like a gingerbread house and relief washed over me like a warm wave.

"It looks beautiful!" Lovisa exclaimed. "Exactly what I imagined."

Mika parked with the boot towards the door. "Super choice! We are really in the heart of nature. Hey, Simone, you beat us!"

In the doorway stood a slight shape, backlit by an enticingly warm interior. "Where have you been? I was freaking out here on my own. This house creaks and groans and my nerves are shredded after two hours here by myself. What took you so long?"

"Same old Simone," I muttered.

We got out, stretched our stiff limbs and dragged our bags indoors. Simone embraced Lovisa and me but reserved her greatest enthusiasm for Mika. Fair enough. She hadn't seen him for two years, whereas we were a regular feature in her life.

"I thought you would have been here hours ago. This place is spooky. There was no one here when I arrived but the code for the key box worked so I could get in out of the cold."

"That's why I shared it with everyone," I said, as sweetly as I could manage. "Whoever gets here first unlocks the place and makes it cosy."

She took the hint and stopped her dramatics. "*Allons-y*, the fire is lit and I made Gael's *mince* pies."

The *mince* pies were an old joke. *Mince* in French means thin. The classic British suet and preserved fruit in pastry scattered with sugar could never be described as 'thin'. We ate them anyway, drank hot chocolate and spread out on the sofas around the fire. I had a good feeling about this place. The bedrooms were on two floors, three up, three down. By mutual agreement, the three women took the first floor leaving the two men the upstairs.

Lovisa wanted to have a bath and Mika said he was making some calls home, so Simone and I started preparing our dinner: an authentic fondue. As the only genuine Swiss amongst us, Simone had chosen the ingredients herself. *Moitié-moitié* cheese mixture: half Gruyère, half Vacherin; little potatoes, crusty bread and fondue seasoning such as garlic, nutmeg and pepper. She donned an apron from the back of the kitchen door and started giving me instructions. It wasn't like I needed telling how to make a fondue, but her bossy tone and the comic French maid design on her apron seemed to fit. I recalled Clark telling me about the sex shop trip, so kept my mouth shut, smiled to myself and obeyed orders.

We chatted with ease as we worked. Simone's ski break with her sister, my escape from the family, the latest in our jobs. Then she took an intake of breath that made me jump. I dropped the knife I was using to cut potatoes with a clatter.

"What's the matter?" I asked, my tone sharper than I intended.

Simone's eyes were huge and her voice was a shaky whisper. "There he is again. Someone is stalking around the chalet. Look, I wasn't imagining things. He's back."

I followed her sightline and saw a dark hooded shape outside the kitchen window. My pulse sped up and I swallowed. "Probably the concierge making sure we got in all right. I'll go and have a word. We don't want anyone lurking about, thanks very much."

I dried my hands and marched into the living room, Simone on my heels. As I did so, a loud banging on the front door made us both start and grasp each other's arms. I looked through the spy hole and recognised Clark's familiar features staring at me.

"Clark!" I exclaimed and threw open the door. "What the hell are you doing peering through the windows and scaring the shit out of us?"

"Hey, guys! Just checking I got the right place before I let the taxi driver go." He turned and gave a thumbs-up to the car idling on the drive. The cabbie tooted his horn and crunched away down the snowy road.

"Come in! We've been messaging you, wondering where you were. Give me a hug."

He did so and released me to embrace Simone. He stood back to take in the design on her apron. "Glad to see you're still rocking that look! Hey, it's great to see you both. It's a hell of a long way out, this place. The driver didn't believe the chalet was even here because it didn't appear on his Satnav. He was sure I'd made a mistake. He was wrong, it looks gorgeous. Look at that fire!" Clark shrugged off his outdoor gear and opened his rucksack. "Where are L and M?"

As if on cue, Mika emerged on the staircase, with Lovisa right behind him, still in her bathrobe. "Clark!" she beamed.

"The one and only. I brought us the most incredible bottle of gin."

Dinner was on hold until we'd done the greetings, cracked open Clark's gin and toasted the fact we'd made it through another two years. When Mika showed Clark upstairs to unpack and Lovisa went to get dressed, Simone and I returned to the kitchen. I noticed she closed the red-checked curtains before recommencing.

Both absorbed in our own thoughts, we didn't talk much. Until out of the blue, while she was rubbing a garlic clove around the *caquelon*, she spoke.

"A Swiss chalet was a good idea, Gael. But there is something very wrong with this one."

When Simone was making a drama, she became high-pitched and easy to dismiss as a diva. When she was serious, her voice dropped, she dispensed with all the theatrics and used few words.

This was undoubtedly serious. I waited for her to continue. She didn't.

Chapter 14: Simone, 2015

I often wondered if I would ever develop that sense of a biological clock, the minutes ticking away and a sense of urgency regarding motherhood. It never happened. I cannot say if that is directly related to the fact that I terminated my first and only pregnancy, or simply a natural state of affairs. Both my sisters have produced children and I quite like my nieces and nephews. More than I like most children at least. Yet they do not fill me with an ache or a longing or even a sense of loss. Mostly, I like seeing them but when it is time to say goodbye, I breathe a profound sigh of relief. My apartment seems like a haven of peace, cleanliness, order and freedom in comparison to my sisters' chaotic households.

My lack of enthusiasm towards becoming a mother turned into a combination of reluctance and dread when the prospect arose of becoming a stepmother. Claude ticked all the boxes: wealthy, handsome, charming, attentive, cultured and widowed. So there would be no ex-wife looking on the horizon, a blight on our glittering future. The only drawback, or perhaps I should say two drawbacks, were his children. From day one, we engaged in fierce competition for Claude's attention. They were around fourteen, maybe fifteen, so not exactly children. The boy was older than the girl, but it was she who was the calculating, sly schemer. Had it not been for her, I might have formed a reasonable relationship with her brother. But it was not to be.

From the moment their father returned home from the office, they demanded all his focus. Some evenings, I was unable to complete a single sentence without interruption until we finally closed the bedroom door. Even then, at the most inconvenient moments, a knock would come or a plaintive call from one of their bedrooms. Usually it was her. I put all my efforts into persuading their father that they should go to boarding school. English boarding schools were suddenly very popular since the success of Harry Potter. They could learn fluent English, practise British sports such as cricket or croquet, polish their manners and have midnight feasts in the dormitories with all their little friends.

Claude could see the logic behind my arguments, but his sentimental side took precedence every time. "They lost their mother at a young age, *chérie*; I cannot send them away from their father." It drove me to distraction. The tough negotiator who played hardball at work, who was never satisfied with second place even playing tennis with friends, was manipulated and played for a fool by two mini tyrants. My respect for him dwindled as did my willingness for any form of intimacy.

As they got older, they grew even more obnoxious. His daughter turned sixteen and I offered to take her shopping, to buy her clothes suitable for a young woman. It was a disaster. She wanted padded bras, high heels, tight trousers and short skirts. Everything I selected was deemed worthy of nothing more than an eye roll. After several hours of bad-tempered disagreement we arrived home with all the elements you would find in the wardrobe of a common prostitute. Worse, she started flirting with her father. Asking his opinion on her clothes, snuggling onto his lap, giggling at the most facile of his comments as if he were a towering wit.

The boy, on the other hand, began lying, claiming all kinds of viciousness on my part. I have no idea how he achieved it but would show his father bruises on his upper arm and accuse me of physical aggression. I never touched the toxic little beast, mainly out of revulsion. Claude was placed in the position of referee. My word against that of his son. The girl would always back her brother and testify against me. Finally, my credit card went missing and on telephoning the bank to report the loss, I discovered huge amounts had been spent on sports clothes, games, concert tickets and an Xbox. I tore his bedroom apart while he was school and found most of the corresponding items. It transpired that he had spent over 9,000 Swiss Francs online, treating himself and his friends courtesy of my account.

The marriage, not the strongest to start with, could not take the strain. We divorced in the summer of 2015 and thanks to a watertight pre-nup and Lovisa's support, I got my settlement and my freedom all at once. I found an apartment ten minutes from Lovisa and embraced the new lifestyle. I never saw Claude or his hateful offspring again.

My preparations for New Year's Eve began in September and no one knew. Lovisa was away on one of her missions, my return to full-time employment was scheduled for January and I told my friends I needed a holiday, to get over the failure of my marriage. Instead, I booked myself six weeks in a clinic outside Zürich. None of the procedures I underwent would qualify as major surgery as I wanted it to appear as subtle as possible. Nevertheless, subtlety costs money. I sold 90% of the jewellery Claude had given me in order to pay for some truly specialist work. After I had healed I spent another month in a wellness centre, investing the same amount of care on my body as I had done my face. By the time I returned to Geneva, I was closer to my twenty-five year old self than I had been for years.

Next I did my research. Thankfully for my bank balance, this required less cash and more time. The file on his company, his partners, his girlfriends, his family and his interests expanded and developed nuance and depth. I pored over his social media presence, making notes on books, music, films and political opinions. Under the guise of reminiscing about the good old days, I invited Lovisa around to dinner twice while she was back in Switzerland. She gave me some very useful insights, although she did not know it. Women have a code of conduct. It is not written or expressed in words but we all know it and abide by its tenets. If you confide any kind of personal detail in another woman, she is duty-bound to reciprocate. It may not be the same subject or problem but the intimacy of friendship is bound by the same laws as the intimacy of sex. Quid pro quo. I talked about my fear of never pleasing a man in bed. How I had dressed up for Dhan as his French maid and exaggerated my accent, how I had overcome my embarrassment regarding oral sex with Jacques, and how the constant threat of interruption had rendered my private life with Claude a tense and unsatisfying experience.

If I believed in an almighty presence bestowing personal qualities on an individual, I would say Lovisa got my share of the maternal instinct. She was sympathetic and kind, offering advice in a generic sense. When I pressed her for personal experience, playing the flustered and embarrassed naïf, she talked about some of her encounters while working as a volunteer and eventually alluded to a few lessons she had learned in her first serious relationship. Finally, I struck gold.

This time, I was going to get it right.

I had spotted Mika on the first day at university, but I got distracted. All those handsome third-years, each accomplished, sophisticated and about to take on the world, were irresistible. I was a hummingbird drawn to blossoming flowers. Chasing after the impossible, I missed the potential in my own year. After one short-lived flirtation and another embarrassing series of dates, it struck me these men were after bigger fish and I should work my own pool. When I did pay attention to my peers, Clark stood out in terms of looks and physique. I invited him for coffee to discuss the difficulties of translating a literary text. The moment I heard him speak French, I crossed him off my list and wondered how soon I could escape. Then Dhan shoved his way into our conversation, with his charm and his eyebrows and his compliments.

His French was worse than Clark's, but he made me laugh. By the time he introduced me to Lovisa and Mika, we were already a couple, as were they. Mikhael Vakala, first son of one of the wealthiest families in the Czech Republic. Tall, wiry and softly spoken as he was, I wondered how he could be friends with the boisterous Dhan and extrovert Clark. He ticked every box, apart from the single one, but that was a matter of time. I had to do everything in my power to bring us together. It was meant to be.

The first time I actively made a pass at Mika was when we were in Kefalonia. Clark, Mika and I sat on the beach long after Gael and Lovisa had departed. I said I was cold and curled up beside him. He put his arm around me and pulled me close while arguing with Clark about the war in Iraq.

Later that night, I crept into his room. He said no. It was too soon and he couldn't bear to hurt Lovisa. I cried and asked him if he found me attractive because maybe one day ... He said maybe, guided me out of his room and locked the door.

In Berlin, I didn't even try because Gael's sister was all over him like some kind of nasty rash. When we all attended the ten-year anniversary of our intake in Geneva, I asked him outright if there could ever be something between us. We were outside on a balcony and I was wearing a golden body-con dress which proved to everyone nothing had changed. Mika is such a decent man. He held me, kissed me on both cheeks and said he didn't know. That only increased my determination.

I dated Jacques for a few months, whom everyone loved except me. Then there was Claude, whom everyone hated except me. This year would be different. It was my turn to organise and I had chosen a beautiful apartment just a few steps from the Trevi Fountain. Via Gael, I knew Mika's last relationship had failed because his Czech chick wanted children and he did not. I was single, he was single and the time was right. In two years' time, we would all be forty. It was time to accept the inevitable and acknowledge that our history bound us together. Our troubled past would make our perfect future. Who else could make him as happy as me?

Rome was the perfect backdrop to a seduction. I chose the location, I spoke the language, I planned the restaurants and I allocated the rooms. This was my time. We wandered through the alleyways of Trastevere, we took a cab to the peak and looked over the five hills of Rome; we ate pasta in Piazza Navona, drank limoncello in the shadow of the Coliseum and danced around the statues as the bells struck midnight. I linked arms with Clark and Mika as we admired the way Lovisa and Gael threw themselves around the square with their respective partners.

It was two in the morning by the time we found our apartment by the Trevi Fountain and tramped four floors up, everyone exhausted in the happiest kind of way. Gael and Clark fell onto the sofa, curled up in each other's arms and giggling at something or other. I suggested another bottle of champagne to general cheers. Lovisa was the first to surrender to bed. She kissed us all and wished us once again a happy New Year. We closed the door to the living room so as not to disturb her. I kicked off my shoes, my feet tired from dancing and tramping the streets. I poured champagne into four glasses and presented Gael and Clark with one each. Mika was standing by the window, staring out at the view. I handed him his glass, we toasted the advent of 2016 and smiled into each other's glassy eyes. To my annoyance, he took his glass and collapsed onto the sofa on the other side of Gael.

Clark was proposing another toast. "To my chosen family. To our dad, Mika. He's the grown-up we all want to be. To Lovisa, our mom, who nurtures us like her own chicks. To Gael, the big sister we love. To Simone, our little sister who arranged this fantastic Roman weekend. And to me, the adopted American made to feel at home. Cheers!"

I moved across the room and sat on the arm of the sofa next to Mika. We toasted one another, argued about Clark's descriptions of us and leaned in to a comfortable space. My cheek rested on Mika's shoulder and the knuckles of my left hand brushed his knee. I yawned and looked over my shoulder at the three of them.

"I'm ready for bed. It's been a wonderful day and thank you so much for being here. This has not been an easy year for me so to say goodbye in your company is wonderful."

Clark clambered to his feet and held out his arms. "Give us a hug, Simone. Great location, great apartment, great night. Sleep well and see you in the morning."

Gael blew me a kiss. "Goodnight, princess. Happy New Year and thank you for bringing us all to Rome."

I blew a kiss back and looked at Mika with a meaningful stare. He rose to his feet and took my face in his hands.

"Our lovely Simone. You look prettier than ever. Go, get your beauty sleep and thank you for a memorable evening." He kissed me on the forehead, as if I was his niece. I looked at him from under my lashes.

"Goodnight, everyone," I said and slipped out of the living room door. I pulled it closed after me but kept the handle down, so that it remained the smallest bit ajar and waited to hear if Mika would say his farewells and follow. Inside the room, there was silence.

Then I heard Gael's voice, speaking sotto voce. "You missed

your cue there."

Mika dropped his voice too. "I know."

Clark started laughing but he too spoke quietly. "Oh man. What do you want? An embossed invitation?"

I heard Mika's voice, back to full strength. "What I do want? A tequila slammer!"

Gael shrieked with laughter. "A tequila slammer? How old are you?"

Feet thundered away from me and into the kitchen. The refrigerator jangled open and Clark shouted, "We're never too old!"

I closed the door and went to bed. I didn't lock my room but already knew I would not be disturbed.

Chapter 15: Gael, now

Once all the ingredients were prepared, I left Simone in the kitchen boiling potatoes while I set the table. The decorations were all-out Swiss, with lined bread basket, white napkins embroidered with edelweiss, a classic Swiss white wine – Chasselas – an old favourite, a bottle of kirsch to aid digestion, red fondue forks and plates with an Alpine cow motif. The caquelon itself, still in the kitchen, was also bright red with a Swiss flag border around the rim. The mise en place was going to look like some kind of still from an in-flight magazine designed to tempt people to the mountains.

Clark came downstairs first and whistled when he saw my handiwork. "The only thing that's missing is your dirndl!"

"Now there I draw the line. But you can get your lederhosen out if you want."

Simone stuck her head out of the kitchen with a frown. "We're in Switzerland, not Munich and this is hardly the Oktoberfest."

"Sorry, madame!"

She gave a nod and withdrew to the kitchen.

Clark looked at me, stretching his ears from his head. "Hearing of a bat," he whispered. "Right, I'll get some more logs in from outside."

I knew he'd be disappointed that the chalet had a whole wall of firewood-ready logs stacked against the wall. Outdoor Man wanted to chop them himself.

Mika came charging down the stairs while Clark was collecting wood. His energy and restlessness always brings an electricity to the room. "Wow! Look at this! Authentic or what? I'd better go check Simone's not messing up the fondue. She should have waited for the expert."

"You're going to end up getting stabbed with a fondue fork," I warned him as he disappeared into the kitchen.

I took a minute to run upstairs and change into something not-grey or made of jersey, and smeared a lick of Vaseline over my eyebrows, which was as far as my make-up routine went. The smell of melted cheese permeated the whole house and I couldn't wait to eat. I rushed back down and opened the first bottle of wine for an aperitif as Mika returned from the kitchen with an earthenware bowl of potatoes.

"Seems she has everything under control. Dinner's up in two minutes," he said, lighting the warmer to keep the fondue bubbling. He looked up with a smile as Lovisa descended, her nose lifted to inhale the air, dressed in a blue and white trouser suit. The Ice Queen of C&A.

Clark came through the front door with a huge basket of logs, his hair covered with a light dusting of snow. "It's so quiet out there! You can almost hear the snow falling."

Simone carried in the caquelon and we set it on the frame, adjusting the heat to keep the cheese bubbling. It smelt blissful now, but tomorrow morning, it would be a different story.

As always, the first evening together was an opportunity to catch up and reconnect with each other's lives. Clark asked Lovisa about her job, which was a smart move. Because she does such sobering, meaningful work, it always puts a downer on the frivolities of the evening if we get around to discussing that after a couple of bottles of wine. She knows better than to go into the nitty-gritty of what she's up against and keeps it upbeat, but real.

Then Simone asked Mika about his stratospheric success, which opened the floodgates. I'd heard it already and wanted to get on to something more gossip-worthy, but Mika's passion for his subject was endearing.

We stuck bread cubes or potatoes onto our forks, stirred them into the cheese and ate. A fondue needs a rhythm, someone should always be stirring. So Clark did double duty while Mika was explaining the reasons why his app had taken off. I fetched the wine from the fridge and played waitress. When I returned, Simone was telling the others about the man she had met.

"Ooh, goody, we're finally talking about sex," I said, taking my place.

Simone laughed. "No sex. At least not yet. It's a difficult one because we work for the same organisation. What's that expression about dipping your ink? Anyway, I find him great company and he's asked me to accompany him to Milan in January to assist on his refugee council presentation. That might be the moment." Her cheeks were pink and the light in her eyes was less femme fatale and more love-struck.

"Hooray for Simone getting her leg over!" I cheered. "What's his name?"

She giggled. "Vincent. You'd like him, Gael; he has a similar sense of humour."

Clark bounced out of his chair to fiddle with the chalet's iPad.

"Poor bugger. Clark, what is the matter with you tonight? You're up and down like a fiddler's elbow. Leave the music alone, it's fine. I thought you liked Alanis Morissette."

"Listen, I like this album as much as the next bloke, but I fancy listening to something a bit more contemporary. Did you hear the Leonard Cohen one his son completed after his death? Awesome, seriously."

The pace of eating slowed as the weighty combination of cheese, bread and potato did its work. Mika scraped up the 'grandmother', the coagulated cheese at the bottom of the caquelon. He was welcome to it. We finished with a digestif as the conversation turned to politics and we managed to argue for over an hour despite all having exactly the same opinion. Satisfied that we had put the world to rights, the non-chefs cleared the table and we all retired to the huge sofa to recline and moan about how stuffed we were. Clark switched the iPad off and plugged his phone into the stereo instead.

Next thing I knew, Lovisa was shaking my shoulder. "Gael, it's bedtime."

"Already? I thought we were listening to music!"

"We were, but your snoring got too loud. Simone has already gone upstairs and I didn't want to leave you on the sofa. Come on, let's go."

Mika pulled the grate across the fireplace and looked over his shoulder with a grin. "Tomorrow is another day!"

I grunted but gave him a goodnight kiss on the cheek, poured myself a glass of water and followed in Lovisa's footsteps. Whose idea was it to have a fondue?

Chapter 16: Clark, 2017

At university, I had the reputation of a hound dog. It wasn't undeserved. From the minute my feet touched European soil, I was determined to make up for lost time. Putting a horny nineteen-year-old Europhile in the middle of the continent was like putting a hungry bear in a salmon pool. I stuffed myself senseless on all it had to offer. The geography, the names, the museums, the cafés, the culture, the food, the languages, the people and the architectural miracles that made me weep. Have you ever cried while looking at a building? During my gap year, I left a tear-stained trail through London's Tower Bridge, Notre Dame Cathedral in Paris, the Brandenburg Gate in Berlin, and Milan's Duomo to the Alhambra in Spain. Magical, historic places which held stories I had only observed via the medium of TV. As far as I was concerned, sex was another form of exploration and I wanted to discover it all with whoever was game. There were plenty of volunteers. After that night in Montreux, I got worse. Or maybe I got better. No opportunity wasted. Almost as if to prove his rejection hadn't hurt.

I stopped sleeping with men in the year 2001. It wasn't a conscious decision, like becoming vegetarian or something like that, I just lost the urge. My libido dried up completely that year, as the whole exercise seemed completely banal after Dhan's death. The next time I got back in the sack happened to be with a woman and although I've found men attractive since then, I don't want to sleep with them. The only time I came close, the event freaked me out for months afterward.

At a conference in Hong Kong, I sat next to an older Australian guy. I've always liked Aussies and their direct approach. This man had a fun sense of humour and we hit it off. When he gave me his card, I tried not to gape. He headed up a major financial institution, had huge influence over South East Asia and had international business journalists hanging on his every word. He invited me for a drink at the end of the day and I accepted, hoping for a chance to impress and in what would probably be a brief networking opportunity.

We drank a couple of beers in the bar and he mentioned he was working on something huge and such a game-changer in the world of currency exchange, it was kept under wraps. Did I want to come up to his room for a sneak preview? Yep, I was that naïve. He pounced on me in the elevator, pressing his forearm against my collarbone and grabbing my crotch with his right hand. I tried to back away but there's not much room in a private penthouse elevator. He told me it was my lucky day and tonight I was his bitch. Then he bit me. He actually bit me, sinking his teeth into my cheek. The shock and pain overcame any residue of respect for his status and I socked him in the eye. He fell backwards and we stared at each other, panting. He told me I would regret that for the rest of my life. A ping announced our arrival and the elevator doors opened. I grabbed him by the lapels and threw him out, pressing the button for Lobby followed immediately by Close Doors. He started getting to his feet and pointed a threatening finger at me as those incredibly slow doors eventually closed. There was no question of me reporting him for assault. With the power he had, I would be crushed. I packed in under ten minutes, got a cab to the airport and flew out that night.

Two days later, a dozen pink roses arrived at my desk with an envelope. Inside was an invitation to an exclusive think-tank week in Melbourne as an all-expenses-paid guest. There was a picture of Robert de Niro in *Raging Bull* and on the back, a note. *See you there for Round Two?*

Ignoring the whistles and comments, I walked down three floors to reception and gave both receptionists six roses each. On the first floor, well away from my smirking colleagues, I shredded the envelope, invitation and picture. I never heard from him again.

In 2017, the obligation to arrange our twice yearly gathering fell to me. By that time I'd been in London working for an investment bank for three years. When I relocated from Paris, I told myself I'd visit all those places I'd heard of but never seen. The Lake District. Ireland. Cornwall. Liverpool. Cardiff. Edinburgh. In three years, I worked so hard I got no further than Cambridge and only then for a day trip. The answer fell into my lap. Edinburgh for Hogmanay!

In those days, much of my life was spent on trains. My bank had branches in Paris, from where they head-hunted me, Amsterdam, Luxembourg and London. Flying seemed faster on paper but in reality trains were more efficient. You simply get on, find your seat, set up your laptop and start working. At the other end, a short taxi ride to your destination. No security, no queues, no buses to the aircraft and a buffet car for when you want it to stretch your legs. Some of my best work came out of a first-class carriage on the Eurostar.

That's why I chose the sleeper train to Edinburgh, the old romantic in me tipping the decision. I had plenty of time to make my way north because I booked the whole two weeks off but I got on that train at eight p.m. on 26 December. My plan was to become a local, find the best pubs and restaurants in order to play the host. The apartment I rented for the gang was not available until the thirtieth so I found a hotel for three days. The anticipation as I boarded the train made me bounce on the balls of my feet as I stared up at the vaulted ceiling. Inside, I was a little boy, off on an adventure. OK, so it wasn't the Orient Express. But I had a private sleeper cabin to myself and a minuscule en-suite bathroom. Better still, there was a first-class dining car which required one to dress for dinner. Hell yeah, sign me up for that.

Suited, shaved and booted, I turned up for my reservation at eight p.m. The car was pretty full and the attendant asked if I would mind sharing. I looked into the waiter's eyes and could see his desperate plea. His dark eyes and eyebrows curved into a tilde and reminded me of someone.

"Sure," I said. "I can speak a few languages and get on with most people. All part of the adventure."

The waiter's shoulders sagged in relief. "Thank you, sir, would you come this way?"

I passed several tables filled with lively parties and few couples conversing under in muted tones. At the end of the carriage was a table set for two with an elderly lady examining a bread roll. She raised her gaze and took me in, finally looking into my face with a smile. She spoke with a soft accent which reminded me of wool.

"Why, that'll do nicely. Thank you, Hamish."

Mrs Campbell was exceptional company. She only stopped asking questions to eat her food, but otherwise kept up a constant barrage of enquiries. It quickly became apparent that unless I interrupted with questions of my own, the evening would be an inquisition. The gentlest, softest inquisition imaginable, but I had gotten tired of the sound of my own voice.

"Mrs Campbell, I'm sorry to interrupt. Would you mind if I ask you about yourself? For example, where you come from in Scotland? Do you have family? If you don't find it intrusive, I'd like to hear a little bit about your life. I have a feeling it's going to be more interesting than mine."

She told me her stories and kept me enthralled for hours. The dining car emptied and we still sat under a small pool of light while she transported me through her extraordinary adventures. The waiter came for a third time and asked if there was anything else we needed.

"No, thank you, Hamish. You're all right to go to bed. This young man and I have had a fascinating evening and I'd love to do it all again. Goodnight, Clark. I want to say that I'm very glad I met you."

"Likewise. You're someone I don't think I will ever forget. Goodnight, Robbie."

She got to her feet and wrapped her shawl around her shoulders. "Sleep tight and enjoy your time in Edinburgh." She pronounced it 'Embra'. Then she turned and looked into my eyes. "If I were you, I'd forget him." On that bombshell, she left.

I tipped Hamish and swayed along the corridor to my compartment, replaying our lengthy conversation to pinpoint which one of my bland responses could have given rise to such a comment. Forget who? Even after cleaning my teeth and washing my face, I was no wiser. I got into bed and in that liminal state of surrender, a memory surfaced.

I'd been at an airport in India, I can't recall which. Bangalore? It had to be at least five years ago, maybe more. The humidity was intense and I was in desperate need of a shower. As soon as those baggage guys delivered my case, I would grab a cab and have it take me to whatever five-star, air-conditioned accommodation the company had booked. The first cold beer from the mini bar was my North Star.

Suitcases took ages to come onto the carousel and I walked the length of the arrivals hall just to stretch my legs. Part of Baggage Reclaim was open, so waiting relatives could see their loved ones. Families waved, hopped with excitement and blew kisses. It made a change to those sliding doors at Heathrow. I scanned the eager faces of the reception committee; children, lovers, grandparents and there, right in the middle, stood Dhan. He was on his phone, his focus on the floor as he shifted from foot to foot. The same impatient Dhan. At that moment, he lifted his gaze and our eyes met. He stared at me for two seconds and then ducked away into the crowds.

I took off, forgetting my bag and ran towards the Exit. Customs Officers stopped me. Of course they did. Trying to sprint through Nothing to Declare? What an idiot. They let me go eventually; I retrieved my bag after one more check and went in search of a cab, berating myself for a list of failures. Racism: you see an Indian man who looks a bit like someone you once knew and assume it's your dead friend. Assumption: seeing recognition in the guy's eyes which was probably more like 'Why is that weird bloke staring?' if you think about it. Imagination: thinking you can run through the airport like James Bond and recover your mate from the dead.

Here and now, somewhere in the Lake District, the rhythm of the train rocked me to sleep and by the time I awoke for breakfast, I had forgotten all about Doppelgänger Dhan.

Chapter 17: Gael, now

Cheese dreams are the worst. All that bread, fat and potato sat in my stomach like cement and the kirsch, supposedly an aid to digestion, only got me drunk. Around three in the morning, after lying there like a cheese-filled sea slug, I got up to go and make myself peppermint tea. Everything was silent and I turned on the hob light on the stove to give myself the bare minimum of illumination. I wrinkled my nose at the lingering smell of garlic and cheese so opened the window while the water boiled. I drank my tea at the kitchen table.

Overeating and drinking too much weren't the only reason for my wakefulness. In the back of my mind, something was bugging me.

That's the problem with my brain. If something doesn't add up, it will irritate and annoy me until I devote my full attention to the issue. The second problem is that I have an exceptional memory for detail. All good qualities for a journalist, you might think. Except that the details I remember are things like the Italian word for tissues or George Michael's real name: *fazzoletti* and Georgios Kyriacos Panayiotou, just in case you're interested.

The other things I remember are a snatch of conversation which usually proves relevant to nothing at all. The conversation currently buzzing around my brain was one held in a Czech police station, two days after Dhan's disappearance. I closed my eyes and recollected the scene.

A small pale green room, four chairs, and overhead fluorescent light. Opposite me, an unsmiling policeman in plainclothes. Beside me, a tired-looking young guy in a leather jacket who had the thankless task of being our interpreter. So many questions. And I was the one they had least interest in. We went over the timings, we discussed the lights, we confirmed the order of who jumped when and I repeated the answers I'd given him first time around. Then he asked me how long Lovisa and Mikhael had been a couple. Did I think they had a strong relationship? I told him they got together in our first semester, which meant they'd been lovers for over two years, and yes, their relationship was rock solid. The police officer shrugged and said something as an aside to the interpreter, who shook his head in a gesture of sympathy. The cop addressed me again.

"The detective says you're free to go and thank you for your time," the interpreter told me.

The cop got to his feet and held out a hand. I shook it and he left the room. The interpreter gave me a weary smile.

"What did he say to you just then?" I asked.

"That you're free to go," he replied, stretching his long arms towards the ceiling.

"No, just before that. He asked me about the relationship, and then said something to you, which you didn't translate. I just wanted to know what he said."

"Oh, that. It was nothing. He said he hoped you were right because bad luck comes in threes. Your friend Mikhael lost a lot of money in a scam investment and now he loses a friend in an accident at the lake. Take good care of him." He shook my hand and went out of the door, leaving it open so the smells of coffee, cigarette smoke and damp clothes washed into the space. I drained my plastic cup of water and followed him out, going in search of my friends. A scam investment and a friend in the lake.

The two things were not unconnected.

"My plan was to challenge him on New Year's Day. But what I had in store was a bit more than some probing questions. I wanted revenge."

And Lovisa? I snorted with laughter. Lovisa. The Madonna of Tampere. She dedicated her whole life to others and would be no more capable of foul play than an earwig. Her brilliance and star student reputation was tarnished after Dhan's deceit, but nobody kills someone over cheating on a French translation. Unless the betrayal of her goodwill combined with the fleecing of her boyfriend ...

"I went looking for Dhan ... I was so angry and hurt, I swear I could have killed him."

In the silence, my mind returned the same old questions I still hadn't answered after twenty years. Why did the lights go out just as I got back to the cabin? Mika was the one who set up the system, including the timer. Why didn't Simone attach a safety band to Dhan? How come no one stopped him jumping in when it went dark and they weren't ready? Why did Lovisa send me back to the house at that precise moment? Did Dhan suspect something was up and that's why he didn't go in the first time? Was that fear I had seen in the group photo?

The fact was that two of them had a very strong motive for wanting Dhan dead.

In which case, were Simone and Clark simply standing by? A pair of innocents presented as absolute proof nothing underhand occurred. And yet ... Clark's one night of passion with Dhan was a loose end. I couldn't see Clark being embarrassed about it. He was proud of the notches on his bedpost. Maybe Dhan regretted it and that caused a rift between best buddies.

If Simone perceived her unwelcome condition as Dhan's fault, that could, at a push, have triggered her to act. But conspiring to kill him in such a horribly cruel way? I'd known these people for twenty years and my theory made no sense. The biggest question of all, where was his body? All we had was Mika's assurance that nothing ever turned up. What did they do with him?

I opened my eyes and shook my head. Too much cheese and an overactive imagination. I finished my herbal tea and left the cup on the draining board. I looked out into the blackness and was comforted to see a light down the road. I didn't remember seeing any habitation on the drive here, but I was glad to know the place wasn't quite as isolated as it seemed.

My room stank of fondue, so I bundled up the clothes I'd been wearing and shoved them outside onto the landing. I got back into bed, made a little pocket in the duvet for my cold feet and willed myself to sleep. Conspiracy theorist Gael might well require a tinfoil hat.

Chapter 18: Mika, now

I'm a pragmatist. I deal in facts. The reason I'm so successful is that I am aware that facts are open to interpretation. One man's faith is another man's fake news. My work is all about context. It may sound dated to you but in my office, we still use the old mantra 'context is king'.

My perception of reality took a major knock two decades ago and it's been a long focused struggle to acknowledge how skewed a view I used to have. It makes me question everything and seek out people whose opinions oppose mine. I need to test, check, recalibrate and constantly maintain a balanced outlook.

Instinct is like having a friend you can trust. You don't see the evidence; maybe you can't. But you trust this voice. This inner voice guarantees it has your back. And then one day, it doesn't. That can shake your world view and make you doubt everything you ever believed.

Many European languages and cultures place a special significance on the number three. Whether that is the holy Trinity, three witches, an Englishman and Irishman and a Scotsman walk into a bar, good things come in threes, knock three times or education, education, education. There's also the concept of a trio when it comes to bad luck. The new millennium whacked me with one after another. The tragic death of a friend, for which I held myself partially responsible.

The loss of my trust fund and consequently, my privileged position. Worst, the breakdown of a relationship I believed would last a lifetime. Each of these things would not have happened without poor judgement on my part. My instinct was not to be trusted.

Yet even though it had betrayed me, my instinct stuck around. It was the reason I pursued the translation app and recovered all the money I had lost times ten. The lesson I had learned was unlikely to be forgotten. Listen to your instinct. Then test, check, recalibrate and refine until a gut feeling becomes a theory and the theory becomes a practice. Only then can I honour it with my trust.

A gut feeling bothered me from the minute we agreed on an Alpine chalet for the 2019 celebrations. I examined my discomfort. Maybe it was the proximity to Geneva, which held such significance for each of us. Maybe it was the seclusion, high in the mountains, far from other people. Or perhaps it was simply the snow, the cold, the ice. Wherever we had celebrated our reunions on New Year's Eve, we sought out warmth and water or a city so busy you didn't notice the cold. It was ridiculous, if you thought about it. Individually, we often spent winter holidays skating, skiing, snowboarding or even staying in an igloo. But as a group we avoided the ice.

It did me good to spend some time with Gael and Lovisa before we drove up to the mountains. Gael is like me, a pragmatist. Lovisa has convinced herself that she too has a purely practical perspective. She hasn't. At the end of the day, she's a tightly swaddled bundle of emotions, protecting no one more than herself. That is partly my fault. We were so convinced our bond could never be broken, it shocked us both when we found that not only could it break, it could never be repaired.

No one else knew we were trying for a baby. Our pact was to say nothing until Lovisa had passed the first trimester. Only then would we announce our news and activate the plans we had hatched for our perfect future. All the answers to the inevitable questions such as 'Aren't you too young?', 'How will you manage?' and 'Are you sure about this?' were already prepared. We were soul mates and would never love anyone else the same way as we did each other.

But Lovisa miscarried once, twice, three times and on each occasion, we contained our heartbreak in private. It sounds strange but a positive pregnancy test, for me, was a little like being drunk. I was intoxicated by optimism, invincible and buoyant on visions of our future. Then the mother of my almost-child would emerge from the bathroom, her face white, eyes red and shake her head. That's when my hope-hangover would kick in. *How stupid have I been? Why are we deluding ourselves? That is the last time I dare to believe.*

Her cycle, which we both knew better than our study timetable, meant that she would be fertile during the last few days of the year. It seemed like a sign. We would make love in my home country and conceive a child in the final days of 1999 or the bright new start to the millennium. I would recover my financial status, we would graduate before the baby was born and start our lives as a young family filled with hope and happiness.

Of all the things that happened in the aftermath, knowing that Lovisa arranged the termination of Simone's pregnancy cut the deepest. Some things I can never forgive.

In my heart, I still hold a lot of love for Lovisa. She accepted our dreams had gone up in smoke and never tried to rebuild them. I hope she's happy.

Although we made good time, crossing through France and re-entering Switzerland on the Alpine side, Simone had arrived at the chalet before us. Worst-case scenario. If there's one person I know who cannot be alone, it is Simone. She was already nervous and jumpy by the time we arrived. As usual, Gael rolled her eyes, I changed the subject and Lovisa adopted her mantle of Mama Hen. My discomfort towards the chalet lessened as I took in the scale and atmosphere of the place. The kitchen was huge with a separate dining area featuring a chunky wooden table in the centre. The living room could have accommodated twenty people, with long leather sofas, sheepskin rugs, wooden beams and a fireplace the size of a Smart car.

The reunion couldn't really begin until Clark arrived and we still had received no response to our messages. We lounged around drinking hot chocolate and eating cakes for an hour and then I wanted to explore. The chalet was both authentic and modern. Wooden walls and roofs with under-floor heating, traditional throws on top of winter duvets and power showers in every bathroom. Built into the slope of the mountain, the place had ski access from the top floor. I offered to take one of the bedrooms on that level, along with Clark, when he arrived. It suited me perfectly. Some distance from the living area and on the same level as the ski exit. My spirits rose as I unpacked and tried making some calls to Bratislava. The connection was unreliable but I did manage to wish my team a happy New Year.

Because of my height, I always travel with my own blanket. Regular duvets, sleeping bags, throws and so on always fall short. Not only that, but they are usually too hot. That's the reason a handmade cotton blanket accompanies me everywhere I go. That afternoon, I removed the duvet, rolled it into a ball and tucked it into the wardrobe. Then I flapped out my personal blanket and laid it on the bottom sheet. That's how I can be sure that at five o'clock in the afternoon there was nothing in my bed.

Up the stairway squeaks and shouts ricocheted off the wooden walls. Out of the window, tail-lights of a taxi were disappearing down the lane. Clark must have arrived. I put on my slippers and made my way downstairs, a smile already spreading across my face. Lovisa emerged from her bedroom in a bathrobe, pink and moist as if from a seashell, her face as happy as my own. We hurried downstairs together to say hello to Number Five.

We greeted, we acclimatised and we drank gin. I showed Clark his room and left him to unpack. I ducked into my own room to check my phone which was on charge and returned downstairs.

After a wonderful evening of laughter and companionship and far too much cheese, we had reconnected. Clark displayed his usual energy, jumping up to change the music almost every other track. The fire, travelling and heavy meal weighed on us all, so one by one we made our way upstairs to fall into our respective beds. I cleaned my teeth, slightly drunk, fondue stuffed and content. These occasions, which I nearly always dread, do something good for my soul. I turned off the light, pulled back my blanket and just before I got into bed, I noticed something glinting in my mattress. The curtains were open, and the moon shone through the window. I picked up what looked like a coin, my brain slow to make sense of this silver disc lying on the sheet. Reaching for the lamp, I flicked on the switch and saw I was holding a chocolate coin encased in silver. On my bed there were many more in various different sizes.

Unease penetrated my muddled mind. Collecting them all together I placed them in a pile on the bedside table. Then I counted. There were thirty. Thirty pieces of silver.

Mouth dry and skin prickling, I checked under the bed, in the wardrobe, outside on the hallway, in the equipment cupboard and in the bathroom. I double checked the lock on the exit to the ski slope. Everything was as it should be. I returned to my room, locked the door and closed the curtains. Then I lay under my handmade blanket and stared at the ceiling in the darkness.

Chapter 19: Gael, now

As a result of my night-time cogitations, I was up last. The others were all in the kitchen, drinking coffee and eating yet more bread. Lovisa handed me a glass of orange juice.

"How did you sleep?" she asked.

I blinked at the table. "You are not telling me you bunch of maniacs are having cheese for breakfast? After last night? I'm never eating or drinking ever again."

They all laughed and Simone pushed the plate of cheese and ham slices towards me.

"You need to load up on proteins and carbs before skiing," she said.

"Stuff protein, stuff carbs and bollocks to skiing," I said, pouring myself a coffee. "You know how I feel about winter sports. You go ahead and chuck yourself off the mountainside. Get your noses burnt, break your ankles, see if I care. I'm going to stay here, curled up beside the fire, like the sensible person I am. Something told me this would happen, staying with a bunch of snow bunnies."

Mika placed a hand on my shoulder. "Why don't you at least walk with us to the start of the ski run? It's a beautiful day and you'll feel much better with some fresh Alpine air into your lungs."

"Yes, come with us," Simone encouraged. "We won't be long,

Just a few hours on the slopes this morning. We'll be back by lunchtime, ready to start preparations on the banquet."

"Or," said Lovisa, "you might want to take a drive into town. There are a few more things we need to get and you can take the car. That's OK, isn't it, Mika?"

"Sure. But you don't have to run errands, Gael. I'm happy to go after we finish skiing. Lovisa has already prepared the shopping list."

"Lovisa would," I said, crossing my eyes at her. "Yeah, fine, I'll do the shopping. How far away is the next best thing to civilisation?"

"There's a village about half an hour away, but they're not likely to stock the kind of thing we need. I recommend you drive to Saint-Maurice. They got some decent supermarkets there."

While they all went off to get changed into various shades of pastel ski-suits, I sat at the table, refilling my coffee cup and peeling a clementine I couldn't finish. The chalet was a ski-in, ski-out, which meant they could open the door on the top floor and ski right out across the countryside. I took my coffee up two flights of stairs to join much laughter and clattering and cheered to see them whoosh-whoosh away over the slopes. They did look the part, I had to admit. After waving them off in the sunshine, I closed the door and crossed the landing to look down the lane. Two floors up I should be able to spot the cottage whose light I'd seen the night before. As far as I could see in the sparkling morning sun, no chalet, farm or any other form of habitation was visible.

"Arr, 'twas pixie lights, me dear," I told myself in a cod West Country accent. "The mountain spirits are playing tricks upon a maid." The chill wound its way around my ankles and I returned to the warmth of our kitchen to clear away the breakfast things.

About an hour later, I heard the upstairs door slam shut. Intruders were unlikely in such a remote location, but you could never be too careful. I hurtled up the stairs two at a time. Just inside the doors stood Clark, trying to remove his outdoor gear.

His face twisted in pain. "Ow! Shit!"

"Clark? What happened?"

"I fell, hit my shoulder and it hurts like hell. I can't get this suit off. I'm gonna need your help here, Gael. Can you pull on the sleeve?"

I took hold of the cuff and very gently drew it towards me. Clark winced and he sucked in a breath through his teeth.

I stopped. "OK, this isn't working. How about I hold on tight to the sleeve and you pull away from me? That way, you're in control of how much it hurts."

With much grimacing and foul language, he managed to extricate himself from the top half of the suit. There was a light sheen of sweat on his face and he looked worryingly pale.

"Sit down," I said, and guided him to one of the wooden benches. I ran downstairs again to fetch a slug of brandy and set to work removing the bottom half of his suit and his ski boots. "There. Do you think you need to see a doctor?"

He shook his head. "I don't think it's dislocated, just a torn muscle. I'm gonna take a hot shower. Could you help me take this top off?"

With great care, I slipped off the silken undershirt he was wearing and helped him to his feet. "Here's the plan. I'll wait till you get out of the shower and see how you feel. If you're better, I'll leave you here and go do the shopping. If not, you'd better come with me and see if we can find a doctor."

"Yeah, thanks. Do you think you could find me some painkillers? I didn't bring any."

"Of course. Lovisa always brings a full medical cabinet wherever she goes."

Sure enough, in the bathroom on the first floor, I located Lovisa's sponge bag and next to it a white plastic box with a red cross on the front. When Clark emerged, bare-chested and wearing jeans, I was waiting with two Ponstan Forte and a glass of water. He swallowed them down and faced me.

"The shower did jack shit. It's still agony. This is more than a sprain so I'm coming with you to get this checked out."

Together, we managed to get him zipped into a fleece and a warm jacket. I put his feet into socks and boots and we made our way downstairs and out to the hire car. To my disbelief, the passenger side front tyre was flat. I swore violently and sent Clark back inside while I changed the wheel. There are advantages to being a petrol head.

By the time I had jacked up the car, taken off the wheel and replaced it with the spare, my hands were frozen and filthy. I looked behind me and saw Clark peering through the kitchen window of the chalet. I gave him the thumbs up and out he came, locking the door behind him. Two minutes later we were finally on the road.

Although I drove as carefully as I could, the journey was torture for Clark. Every bump and turn caused him pain. And driving down a snowy mountain road, there are plenty of bumps and turns. When we hit the motorway, things went more smoothly and I asked him to check on his phone for a likely doctor's surgery in Saint-Maurice. As it turned out, we had to go to the emergency room at the small city hospital. I waited with him for half an hour until my stomach started to rumble. I checked the time and was horrified to see it was half past one. The shops were due to close at four o'clock and I still wanted to get a replacement tyre as well as all the shopping. We agreed that I would go and deal with all that crap while he waited to be seen. Then I would collect him and take him back to the chalet.

It seemed the entire population of France had forgotten one crucial element of their New Year's Eve preparations and had all come to Saint-Maurice to buy it. First I had a heated exchange with the guy in the Volvo garage who told me it was impossible to provide a spare wheel at such short notice. I told him that if he didn't it would be on his conscience if I and my sick boyfriend were trapped in a remote chalet with no transport. With extremely bad grace he told me to come back in an hour and took the damaged tyre off my hands.

Next up in the afternoon's never-ending joys was a trip to the supermarket. I drove round and round the car park, waiting for someone to vacate a space. When I spotted one and shot into the spot, I had a ferocious altercation with a guy in a Land Rover who swore he'd been indicating first. But I was already in and ready to physically fight the bloke to keep my spot. He called me an ungentlemanly name and drove off with an unnecessary squeal of tyres. The Co-op was packed, I couldn't find half the ingredients we needed and then I stood in an immense queue, watching the minutes tick away until the garage closed, waiting to pay for my basket full of frivolous, wasteful extras. I may have called Lovisa an ungentlemanly name as I scrunched her list into a ball in my pocket.

Clark sent me a message to say he was ready, but he would have to wait till I'd been to the garage. The bad-tempered owner was even worse tempered because I was late. He also told me there was nothing wrong with the original tyre. It had simply been deflated. He had re-inflated it, tested it and I could take it away. I thanked him and asked him how much it would cost. He waved me away and wished me a happy New Year. The one bright spot in a litany of miseries.

The second bright spot was Clark. He had indeed dislocated his shoulder, but the doctor had been able to realign the joint, give him some heavy duty painkillers and put his arm in a sling. It meant he would not be able to drink alcohol as well as take the pills, but he should recover in a couple of days. It was getting dark by the time we left Saint-Maurice and we messaged the others to let them know we were en route. We had eaten nothing since breakfast and were starving hungry. I stopped at a petrol station and bought us each a slice of quiche and a bottle of water, which did wonders for lifting our mood.

I turned off the motorway and took the turning to the little village, passing through towards the forest and up the mountain. If the journey out had seemed torturous, the return trip seemed twice as long in the dark. I put the lights on full beam and drove cautiously along the narrow lanes. This was not my idea of fun. I recalled the previous day, when Mika had driven this route, also in the dusk with not a word of complaint.

Clark hadn't said a word since we finished scoffing our snack, allowing me to concentrate on driving in these conditions. Then he spoke.

"Gael, I need to tell you something."

"What?" I asked, wishing whatever it was could wait for another time.

"You know I had a lot of casual sex back in the day."

My mind whirred around a well-worn track. Clark was going to tell me he was HIV positive.

"Back in the day?" I asked, with a smile, but didn't take my eyes from the terrain ahead.

"Touché. The truth is a lot of that was compensating for the fact I couldn't have the one I wanted. For three years, I was obsessed with the same person and I knew, even though there was love between us, it was a different kind of love."

"Before I pull over, burst into tears and propose, you're not talking about me, right?"

He gave a sad little laugh. "No, I'm not talking about you. I think the love we have for each other is mutual. I gotta say, though, the couple of times we ended up in the sack ..."

"... do not need to be resurrected. I swear to God, Clark, if you start giving me points out of ten, you can walk from here." I changed down a gear to crawl up the hill. "I think I know who it was. Our absent friend. Let me guess, this started after the weekend in Montreux."

Clark said nothing until we had crested the slope and taken

another bend. "Yeah, I was crazy in love with my straight flatmate. What a loser, right? The thing is, my feelings had been there all along, I guess. Montreux was the one time, just one, when I thought he might feel the same way. We got drunk, high and screwed each other senseless after that Morissette gig. Next morning, he wanted to forget it ever happened. In a way, so did I. To have a taste of what might have been and for him to reject the idea out of hand completely crushed me. He broke my heart and the shagathon that resulted over the next few months was all his fault."

We didn't speak for a few minutes, both thinking back to those days we had believed were halcyon.

"I sort of suspected you had stronger feelings for him," I ventured. "Why tell me? Why now? I'm guessing no one else knows what happened at the jazz festival?"

"Unless Dhan told anyone, and I think that's unlikely … what the fuck!"

We rounded a sharp corner and something huge and dark came barrelling out of the forest directly towards us. I couldn't even make out what it was, but it looked like a giant snowball stuffed with branches, leaves and earth. In the second before we collided, both my feet hit the floor as I slammed on the brakes and wrenched the steering wheel to the right. The tail of the vehicle skidded left and hit something which bounced off the bodywork with a bone-shaking thud. We came to a halt in a snow drift, the headlights smothered by snow.

"Are you OK?" I asked, my voice shaky.

Clark released a long breath. "Just about. Are you?"

"Think so. But whatever that was is definitely not OK."

I put on the hazard flashers. Clark tried to open his door but it was wedged hard against a wall of snow. With a curse I reversed and, thanks to the winter tyres, got some kind of traction. We were back on the road. I looked in the mirror, peering into the glow offered by my reversing lights but could see no sign of life. Clark dug around in the glove compartment. He found a torch and first-aid kit. We got out and scrambled to help the person or animal we had hit. I ran back to the point of impact where you could see the tyre marks of the skid and detritus of leaves, twigs and snow. On the right-hand side of the road, where we had ended up, there was a tall snowdrift over a metre high. On the left, trees hung over the road and a low bank led into the forest. We paced up and down, shining a torch along the clean white snow that lined both sides of the country road. No injured body, no footprints, no bloodstains and no sign that someone had been there. Clark walked back around the corner to see if the victim had gone the way we came but returned minutes later shaking his head.

"We should call the police," I said. Leaves above our heads fluttered and several splats of snow landed at our feet.

Clark pulled out his phone. "What do I say?" he asked.

"Just tell them what happened. We hit someone or something but we can't find them. I have no idea if they are badly hurt or even dead. The point is, where did they go?"

"Damn it all to hell and back, there's no signal. Does the chalet have a phone?"

"I don't know. But we can't just leave the scene! For one thing, how do we find this place again?"

"Gael, standing here is gonna achieve jack shit. Let's leave a marker so we know where it happened, then get back to the chalet and call the police. The hire car is bound to have one of those emergency triangles. Let's put it here so we mark the location. Come on, I'm freezing my balls off."

We did as Clark suggested and placed the emergency triangle on the side of the road. With one last look in the mirror, I drove us away, fear and cold making me shiver.

When we arrived at the chalet, the other three came rushing out to greet us. They hadn't received our message and were worried sick about where we were. Clark assured everyone he was fine and told them briefly what had happened on the road. Mika donned his coat to check the car for damage, something that hadn't occurred to me. A rental firm penalty was another turd to add to the pile of crap served up on the last day of this decade.

As the driver, I chose to make the phone call. The police officer I reached listened with some interest as I described events and attempted a rough estimation of where the incident had happened. She told me they would send a car to look at the area and would continue on to take a statement from us.

My shakes had increased to the point where I was almost spasming. Lovisa placed a woollen throw over my shoulders and Simone handed me a glass of brandy. It knocked against my teeth as I tried to drink it. Lovisa stoked the fire while Simone poured Clark another brandy. Then they bookended us, one either end of the sofa, their arms gentle around our backs.

We sat there, going over what happened and coming up with explanation after explanation, none of which was rational. The person or animal wasn't hurt and ran into the forest. Except there were no footprints. The person or animal wasn't hurt and ran back down the road to the village. Except we were at least five kilometres from the village, it was freezing and dark. The person or animal was slightly concussed and ran ahead of us to hide in the forest while we were stuck in the snowdrift. Why would anyone or anything do that?

Mika came in, still holding the car keys. "Not a scratch. You know, it might have been a large snow dump, falling from the trees, and it just felt like a collision. Is that possible?"

"No," Clark barked. "Something was moving at speed out of the forest. It was travelling left to right on a horizontal plane. You don't see snow dumps coming. We both saw it and Gael did an emergency brake which landed us halfway into a snowdrift. We hit something. This was not a goddamned snowfall."

I looked up at Clark, whose face was grey. "If you hadn't been there, I would think I'd imagined the whole thing." I registered the glass of brandy. "Are you OK? Should you be drinking when taking super-strength painkillers?"

"I wonder if either of us should be drinking, as the police might want to breathalyse the pair of us. Still, too late now. If it's booze or painkillers, then I've made my choice." He emptied his glass in two swallows. "Right, this is getting us nowhere. We've reported the incident and that's all we can do. You know what? I'm hungry. We'll have to interrupt our celebrations to talk to the police, but we don't have to drop our plans altogether. Mika, you want to get the shopping from the car? It's getting late and if we want to eat before midnight, we should start cooking now."

Subdued and thoughtful, we made our way to the kitchen. Only then did I notice Lovisa's hand in a clean white bandage.

"Not you as well?" I said. "What did you do?"

She shot a quick look at Simone. "Oh, it's just a little cut."

Simone gave me an apologetic smile. "The champagne you put outside. We found it when we got back from the slopes and brought it indoors. The problem was, the bottle had frozen and exploded. Lovisa cut herself when we were clearing up. I expect you thought you would be back much earlier. Déjà vu, *hein*?"

I watched Simone chopping onions and Lovisa washing a bunch of coriander with her un-bandaged hand. The front door slammed and Mika joined us with two paper bags of shopping, followed by Clark with the car keys.

"But I didn't," I said. "I didn't put any champagne outside."

Lovisa shrugged. "Don't worry, Gael. You had a stressful day and probably forgot all about it. No one blames you."

I stared at their backs, both busy and efficient and my incompetence already forgiven.

"No, I didn't forget. Lovisa, Simone, listen to me. I did not put any champagne outside. If there was a bottle outside the chalet when you returned from skiing, someone else put it there. I'm not trying to evade responsibility, but I swear to you, the last thing on my mind this morning was chilling some champagne. I finished breakfast, had a shower, helped Clark out of his ski gear, changed the bloody flat tyre and drove us to town. It never occurred to me to put a bottle of champagne outside in the snow."

A silent conversation was taking place between Mika, Simon and Lovisa. Eventually, Mika spoke. "It wasn't in the snow. It was on the windowsill, just like before."

Everyone froze.

"Wait!" I said. "Which window?"

"The kitchen window," said Lovisa.

I turned to look at Clark, making a face of incredulity.

"What? You think I did it? Standing there with a dislocated shoulder, watching you change a tyre to get me to a doctor and the first thought that occurs is to chill some champagne?"

"No! That's exactly what I mean. When I finished changing the tyre, I looked at the kitchen window to call you to come out to the car." I closed my eyes, bringing the scene to life behind my eyes. "I was looking right at the kitchen window. I saw your face. I gave you the thumbs up. There was no bottle of champagne on the windowsill; I would stake my life on that."

Clark nodded slowly. "You're right."

When weird shit happened – something freaked us out, upset us or reminded us of something we'd rather forget – it was always Lovisa who found the comforting words. This evening, she said nothing.

Eventually, Simone cleared her voice. "Well, in that case, it's obvious what happened. The owner or concierge or manager of this place came up here to check everything was all right. He brought us a bottle of champagne as a New Year's gift. He rang the doorbell but no one answered. We were skiing and you two had gone down to see a doctor. He assumed we'd be back soon and left the champagne on the windowsill so that we would see it on our return. It's just a nasty coincidence that the same thing happened twenty years ago."

Her calm voice had the same effect as the brandy, warming, reassuring and shining a bright morning light on my night-time fears. We all agreed with her rational analysis and set to work chopping, frying, grilling, basting and boiling. Working one-handed, Clark was of limited assistance, so he suggested making us all an aperitif, an idea which pleased everyone. We gave him our orders and conversation warmed as the heat of the kitchen created condensation on the windows. I went into the living room to set the dinner table and met Mika coming through the front door with a basket of logs. He gave me a tight smile.

"You do believe me, right?" I asked. "I didn't even go outside the front door until we left for town. Simone is right. It was just a nasty coincidence."

"I believe you. And I'm sure Simone is right. It is just a nasty coincidence. Made even nastier by the fact that champagne was exactly the same brand as the one that exploded in 1999."

Chapter 20: Clark, now

The whole damn thing was getting under my skin. We should have quit this bullshit ten years ago, if not earlier. What did we really have in common? We spent three years together in the late nineties, that's all. Time to let it all go.

Sure, the chalet was cute. Those ski-in, ski-out places are hard to come by and we had plenty of space to ourselves. But from the minute I arrived, something was wrong. I don't go in for all that aura, sixth sense, esoteric thinking about my subconscious, because mostly that's just a place to dump all the crap you can't deal with. There was something about that chalet, though. From the minute I arrived, my guts told me to get away as soon as I could.

The build-up started before I even got there. Buying all those Indian ingredients brought back memories I'd rather forget. If they were set on spending December 31 every two years in mourning, I'm out. Time to move on and interact with one another as forty-plus adults, not grieving twenty-year-olds. It gets old. Really old, really boring.

When I arrived, Gael began by telling me off and Simone was wearing a French maid pinny. *Plus ça change*. They made fondue, exactly the light, refreshing kind of meal you want to enjoy the night before New Year's Eve excesses. Worst of all, the so-called random music player selected Alanis Morissette every third track. I swear I'm not exaggerating. To me, it felt like a sign. It's over. This would be the last time. We should let it go and get ourselves a life.

The next morning, I was in a better temper, looking forward to some quality skiing and getting out into the Alpine sunshine. The weather was beautiful and the views the kind that physically restored you. Gael stayed behind while the four of us got into our kit, picked what we wanted from the chalet's selection of snowboards, sleds and skis for the different shoe sizes, then struck out across brilliant white snow. It was cold, maybe minus 5° or so, but sunny and clear. I took great lungfuls of pristine, oxygen rich air and remembered how much I loved this country.

We tried a couple of simple runs to get warmed up and it all came back. I hadn't been skiing for two years. Jen felt the same way Cass had about winter sports so my wife and I holidayed in the Caribbean and Morocco instead. I loved the sun but even if I hadn't managed to persuade my first or second wife to join me, I would always love the snow.

Now the muscle memory was kicking in and the pure joy of mastering the elements elated me more than any drug I have ever consumed. Mika and I chose a run with a higher level of challenge. A slalom course. A couple of jumps. A steep descent towards a tree line. My blood was pumping and I could not wait to get started.

We took the ski lift to the top and I went first. There was something about the combination of exhilaration and concentration, body and mind working in partnership, which transcends similar experiences. I knew that when I reached the bottom I would be punching the air and desperate to do it all over again.

That lasted until the first jump. The sun was bright but I had my ski goggles, so vision was not a problem. As I approached the jump, light reflecting from somewhere on the right blinded me for a second. I tilted my head, my attention on the approaching jump, but the light flashed again, flickering across my vision. At that speed, I could do nothing to mitigate its effects and simply trusted my body to judge the leap. The moment my skis left the platform, I was off balance. Sailing through the air for three weightless seconds, my skis hit the ground, skewed right and my left shoulder took the impact.

Mika saw my fall and skied directly down to help me. A steward helped us off the run and made a cursory assessment of my injury. No more skiing that day, she said, and medical attention was urgently required. Mika offered to come back with me but I insisted he continue. All I wanted was a hot shower and some relief for my shoulder. I didn't mention the blinding light. Every skier who falls has an excuse. In retrospect, I wish I had not been such an alpha male and said something at the time.

When we got back to the chalet, my relief to see Gael was still there nearly provoked uncontrolled sobs. I showered in the vain hope that would improve the pain. It didn't so I returned to my room to dress. The room was exactly as I left it, clothes scattered over every surface and the faint smell of fondue in the air. Except for the picture. All over the chalet, there were woodcut prints and pencil sketches and local landscapes. The styles varied but the colours did not. Everything was monochrome. When I had arrived, I noted the pictures in my room and admired the subtle pencil work delineating Alpine roofs. Authentic and local. I approved of both.

One-handed, I pulled on clean underpants and managed to wriggle into my jeans. When I looked up, the pencil sketch on the wall above my bed had been replaced. Instead, there was a printout of a newspaper article. The picture showed a cloud of smoke billowing across the lake.

I recognised it immediately. The fire at the casino in Montreux. The event that inspired Deep Purple's 'Smoke on the Water'. I grabbed the rest of my clothes and shot out of that room, heart thudding, shoulder throbbing, desperate to get away from that place and never come back.

Chapter 21: Simone, now

Sometimes a revelation comes to you in one big flash. Other times, lots of random little details add up to a sum which is more than its parts. While Mika, Lovisa and I stayed in the kitchen to keep an eye on the food, Gael and Clark spoke to the police. We couldn't hear anything because we had closed the door. Nevertheless, none of us said a word. Lovisa moved between hob and the oven, checking every dish. Mika placed a large wooden tray on the kitchen table and quietly assembled all the cutlery, serving dishes and plates. I am sure somewhere in her luggage, Lovisa had table decorations, personalised name plates and other baubles, but that kind of frippery was long forgotten tonight.

I sat at the table studying my fingernails and thinking. Random little details. I focused my mind and concentrated on the number of things that made me feel uncomfortable. There was no point in voicing my fears to the others, at least not yet. They would label me a drama queen, trying to pull the spotlight onto myself. I had to think this through with a rational mind.

When the taxi dropped me here yesterday afternoon, it was snowing. The driver helped me to the porch with my luggage. I paid him the fare and a decent tip because my bags were heavy, naturally. He asked if he should wait until I was inside, but I told him not to bother. There were fresh footprints around the side of the house, so someone had already arrived. I knocked on the door, watching the tail-lights of the taxi drive away. When no one answered I assumed they must have gone exploring, and used the code Gael had sent us to open the little key safe. Sure enough, the key was there and I let myself in.

I checked the chalet for signs of life and found none. No suitcases, no territorial marks claiming a bedroom, nothing. I chose a room I liked and began unpacking. I sent messages to Lovisa and Gael regarding their ETA, but got no reply. Then I carried two bags of groceries downstairs to the kitchen. Outside, the snow had stopped but the light was fading, so I switched on some music and started to bake Gael's favourite, mince pies.

I was trying to work out the cooker when my eyes refocused. In the reflection of the glass oven, I saw a figure at the window, wearing a hood. My breath caught involuntarily and I whipped around. The others refer to me as a drama queen, but I live alone and do not spook easily. The view from the window showed nothing but snow-covered slopes. I was certainly not stupid enough to open the front door and check for footprints, but I did switch on the outside lights. If anyone was hanging about, they would be brightly illuminated. Back in the kitchen, I set the oven to 200°C and beat an egg to glaze my pies. When the others eventually arrived half an hour later, I was so relieved to see them I forgot to check the path around the house.

Random detail number two. The apron. When I pulled it out of the drawer and tied the tapes around my waist, I did not register the pattern. It was only when Clark made a comment about me 'still rocking that look' that I checked in the mirror. A French maid outfit complete with cartoon cleavage and frilly pinafore. The only way Clark could know what I used to wear when role-playing sex games, was because Dhan had been less than discreet. The fact the chalet had a French maid apron I put down to coincidence.

Random detail number three. The mirror. Before Clark arrived, Lovisa had bathed. She came downstairs to greet him in her bath robe. We didn't dress for dinner as everything you wear when eating fondue tends to stink for days. So the first time I entered the bathroom other than to deposit my necessaire was when I cleaned my teeth and performed my skincare routine before bed. I cleansed my face of make-up and applied my moisturiser. Steam from the warm water revealed a message on the mirror. **A +**.

I frowned, assuming it was one of Lovisa's positive mantras, wiped it off with a towel and continued to apply Crème de la Mer.

Random detail number four. The champagne. I thought Gael was telling the truth. She did not put that bottle on the windowsill and neither did Clark. My explanation sounded good but I didn't believe it. If the concierge had arrived to deliver a bottle of champagne and found us absent, he would have used his key and placed the champagne on the kitchen table, probably with a business card. Not even a complete imbecile would leave Möet et Chandon outside in minus 7°.

Random detail number five. When we returned from skiing, we came in via the top door. Skis outside, we took off our gear on the landing. When I went to hang up my ski suit, I noticed the hook I had used that morning was now occupied. When my suit had previously hung was a child's ski suit which had not been there before. I asked Lovisa and Mika if they had seen it, perhaps moved it before we left. They were as puzzled as me.

I'm not paranoid, but something in this chalet stinks and it is stronger than the cheese.

Voices came from the living room and the front door slammed. I drew my attention back to the present. Through the kitchen window, we watched the police car drive down the lane, its brake lights turning the snow pink. We waited. The kitchen door slid open and Gael came to join us.

"They didn't find anything. Their theory is we came across a deer, struck it a glancing blow and it sprang off into the forest. They returned our emergency triangle and told us not to worry about it. We should have a good New Year's Eve but just to reassure us they will check the area again tomorrow morning in daylight. So that, I guess, is that."

Clark slouched into the doorway behind her, his right hand cradling his left elbow in its sling. "They've gone. Shall we eat?"

I looked into Gael's eyes. They seemed dull and tired to me. "Do you believe it was a deer?" I asked.

She shrugged. "No. But for want of a better explanation, I'll run with it. Come on, let's put a truly shitty day behind us and enjoy a decent meal. Who's up for red wine?"

We ate a lot, we drank a lot and we tried, all of us, to recapture some of the bonhomie of the night before. We failed. I racked my brains to think of some kind of game we could play but came up with nothing. I have never been a game kind of person. That would be Gael's forte and she was barely holding up her end of the conversation. Clark's discomfort grew more obvious throughout the evening. He shifted, repositioned, accepted a cushion from Lovisa but was evidently in pain. Gael's introspection became a vacuum and Mika was drinking wine as if it were water. Conversation ran dry and I checked my watch to see how long we had to force ourselves to stay awake. It was ten to eleven.

Into the silence, Mika spoke. "Do you believe in ghosts?"

We all stared at him. Mr Practical asking such a bizarre question? I wanted to laugh. But he did not and neither did anyone else.

"The reason I ask is because I feel like I'm going a little crazy. I know I'm over-thinking this and I ask you just to listen. Ever since we came here, things haven't felt right. Maybe it's because we are all thinking back to twenty years ago. Maybe it's our age, where the past feels longer than the future. I don't know. But the last twenty-four hours have freaked me out and I don't think I'm alone."

Tears of relief pricked my eyes and I reached for Mika's hand. "I am so glad you said that. I understand because I feel exactly the same way. There was no way I could raise the subject, because you would all dismiss it as 'classic Simone'. Something is wrong. To answer your question, Mika, no. I do not believe in ghosts. But I do think someone is trying to frighten us. Who and why and how they know so much, I have no clue."

Chapter 22: Gael, now

From sleepy, disconnected and spent, the atmosphere became charged and weighty. Everyone was wide awake. The change was not positive. I looked from one face to the other, my suspicions hardening into a conviction. It was clear to me these people were haunted. Whatever factors had frightened them, this was more than a memory of a twenty-year-old tragedy. For the first time, I allowed my shapeless suspicions to form a concrete theory.

Mika's house, Mika's lights, Mika's long strong arms hauling me out of the icy water. Mika's lies. He knew Dhan had stolen his money before we went to the Czech Republic. Filled with rage, he wanted revenge.

Lovisa, earth mother, top-level A student, shocked and stressed by Dhan's plagiarism. She confronted him and he laughed.

Simone, the sensationalist. Responsible for the wrist clip to stop any one of us from slipping under the ice. Simone's pregnancy, Simone's hold over Dhan.

Clark's flatmate, Clark's love, Clark's lean, buff arms grabbing my wrists to bring me to safety. Clark's refusal to talk about the events of twenty years ago.

Disclaimer – there's no guarantee that this list is complete. That's just what I could gather over two decades. Maybe there was more?

The four of them, around a hole in a freezing lake. Lovisa sending me back to the house, the lights going out and Dhan, with no preparation, trying to prove himself, like the clown he always was.

I rested my cheek on my hand and stared into the fire. They could not possibly have planned it, but there was every chance when the opportunity arose, they took it. Perhaps they didn't kill him, but simply let him die.

Mika broke the silence. "Perhaps it's time to be completely honest. Lovisa has known for a long time, and I recently told Gael. I loaned Dhan €30,000 as part of a start-up investment in 1998. After his death, I discovered the start-up had failed partly because my money had never reached them. I lost it all. Yesterday evening, when I went to bed, I discovered some chocolate coins under my blanket. Thirty silver chocolate coins. Either Gael or Lovisa has a sick sense of humour, or something strange is going on."

We all looked at one another for an explanation, but none was forthcoming.

Lovisa was shaking her head. "That doesn't make sense. Gael and Simone were cooking the fondue. The first time I went to the second floor was this morning, when we went skiing. I would swear neither Gael nor I would do something as unpleasant as that."

"Please listen to me," Simone asked, her voice low and serious. "I was thinking about this while you were talking to the police and I think Mika is right. Something bizarre is going on. In my heart, I trust all of you, and I ask you to do the same for me. Before you arrived yesterday afternoon, I saw someone looking through the window. I know you think I make these things up but no. Not hysteria, not paranoia, not Simone dramatics. Someone was there. There were fresh footprints in the snow when the taxi driver dropped my bags.

"The champagne bottle left on the windowsill was Moët et

Chandon, just like twenty years ago. The apron in the kitchen has a design of a French maid. Excuse me for giving too much information, but when Dhan and I were into role-play, my costume was a French maid. When we returned from skiing, a child's ski suit was on the hook. That was not there when we left." She looked at Lovisa and Mika for agreement.

They both nodded.

Simone continued. "Either one of us is playing some tricks or pranks to frighten the others, which I cannot believe of any one of you, or someone else has a lot more information than I feel comfortable with."

I looked around the table, each face sharp with concentration. Simone's conspiracy panic attacks were a familiar pattern to me, but I was genuinely surprised at Mika. Unless my theory was right and guilt was catching up with every one of them. I opened my mouth to speak, but was interrupted by Clark.

"Full disclosure. The last two days have freaked me out. Dhan and I were flatmates for two years, but one night, and one night only, we were something more. The night we went to Montreux to see Alanis Morissette, we had sex. We agreed it was a mistake and we would never discuss it again." He gave me an imploring look. I blinked slowly, the only gesture I could think of to reassure him that his secret was safe with me.

"Last night, the music player was programmed to play Alanis Morissette every third track. I checked it this morning before breakfast. When we were skiing this morning, something was shining in my eyes. You know what it's like when you ski, sometimes you do capture a reflection. But this was deliberate. Someone was trying to disorient me by shining a light directly into my eyes. It caused me to fall and dislocate my shoulder."

The atmosphere around the table was so tense that when a log popped in the fireplace, we all jumped. Lovisa laughed and topped up all our glasses.

"We can't let decent wine go to waste," she said. "Clark, please go on."

Clark reached out and tapped his glass to Lovisa's. "Thanks, Mom. When I got back here, one of the pictures in my bedroom had changed. A pencil sketch of the Alps had been replaced by a photocopy of a news story. The story of 'Smoke on the Water', the fire at the casino in Montreux. I didn't know the background to that song until Dhan told me, that night. And I have other questions. How come a brand-new hire car gets a flat tyre? What's with all that weird shit on the road? Gael knows as well as I do that was not a deer. Something bigger burst out of the forest into the middle of a snowy road and we hit it. To be honest, all this shit is freaking me out and I wanna cut it short. I'm leaving tomorrow, guys, I'm sorry."

I couldn't reach for Clark's hand as he was cradling his elbow but I stroked his upper arm. "I understand. I'll drive you to the train station whenever you want to go. And anyone else who's had enough. Maybe this place wasn't one of my better ideas."

Mika fixed Lovisa with an intense stare. "Three of us have had inexplicable experiences. Lovisa, your emotional intelligence is stronger than the rest of us put together. How do you explain this? Are we hypersensitive because of the anniversary, or the remote location or some alignment of the stars? Are our imaginations going wild? Did someone put something in the fondue?"

Lovisa tucked her hair behind her ear and took several deep breaths. "Why now? If our imaginations are creating phenomena we cannot explain, surely that would have happened the year after the event, not twenty years later. In addition, three of you have had peculiar experiences relating to your relationships with Dhan. I have not, and I don't think Gael would connect the incident on the road to losing our friend two decades previously."

I didn't argue with that, although the champagne and the flat tyre seemed bizarre.

"Lovisa, you know ..." Mika started to speak.

He was interrupted by Simone, taking a gasp and clasping her hand to her mouth. Her eyes grew huge, like those of a frightened calf. "I don't think you're exempt, Lovisa. Maybe you just missed the signs. Yesterday evening, when I went to bed, someone had written a message on the bathroom mirror. A+. I don't think that was meant for me."

Lovisa paled, her eyes narrowing. If it had been me to claim such a thing, she would have refused to believe it. But it was Simone. Her golden girl. She couldn't even accuse me as she had already asserted I was downstairs cooking fondue.

"Perhaps," said Lovisa, her tone thoughtful, "there is some guilt presenting itself. Some anger you have not resolved is manifesting itself which you perceive as a malevolent force."

That I could not allow to slide. "Hang on, Lovisa," I said. "I think you had a major amount of unresolved anger against Dhan just before he died. I appreciate you may feel you have worked that out, but to be honest, I find your tone a little patronising. Simone was pregnant. Mika lost thirty grand. I'd say you, me and Clark all had reasons to feel angry as well."

Lovisa's brow furrowed and she narrowed her eyes. "Simone, Mika and I had grievances, yes. How do you and Clark fit in? You lost a drinking buddy?" Her tone was scathing and struck me like a whiplash.

My head grew hot and I drained my wine glass. I would no longer be patronised by this self-styled maternal figure. She knew hardly any of our secrets and it was time for some truths.

"My drinking buddy and on paper only, my husband-to-be."

No one moved. Four pairs of eyes stared at me as if I'd transformed into a witch.

"It was a practical thing, that's all." I kept my tone light. "Dhan's family had arranged him a wife and he could not refuse them. She came from a good family and he looked like a decent catch. He was educated, middle-class and a second-generation immigrant. If he refused, he would have broken his family's heart. The only way he could get out of it was by having her refuse him. And one way of doing that was by becoming a divorcee. He explained the situation and asked if I could help. I've got no hang-ups about the whole institution of marriage, so I said yes. We planned to have a quick registry office ceremony when we were both back in Britain at Easter. But Dhan didn't live that long."

Simone and Clark stared at me, the same question burning in both pairs of eyes. A charge of power shot through me. It only took twenty years and now it was my turn to spring a surprise. I poured more wine, enjoying my moment.

"Like I say, it was nothing more than a practicality. Dhan and I had a lot of affection for one another, but it certainly wasn't sexual." I addressed Simone and Clark. "We never slept together, not even once. In fact, the plan was to file for divorce on precisely that point. Non-consummation of marriage. Quickie divorce, Dhan's reputation irreparably damaged and the bride-to-be would want nothing more to do with him. Dhan's reputation as an impulsive hothead made the whirlwind romance story plausible and his parents would eventually forgive him. Two single Brits, no permission required. I was just doing a good mate a favour."

Simone arched her eyebrows. "A favour for a good mate? Really? Why do I find that hard to believe?"

My anger ballooned into a mushroom cloud and then imploded to a cold tight ball behind my belly button. "Perhaps because you've never had a really good mate? Ask yourself this, Simone, have you ever done anything selfless in your life? You can't believe anyone would do something with no benefit to themselves because you approach people with a transactional mindset. Can this person do something for me? No? In that case, there is no basis for friendship. Simone doesn't have friends, only interests."

As I could have predicted, she recoiled with an intake of breath, welled up with tears and turned to Lovisa. "Why is she being so horrible to me?"

Lovisa placed her hands on Simone's cashmere-clad shoulders with reassuring strokes, which incensed me still further. I took a gulp of wine to fuel yet another broadside but Mika spoke first.

"If someone is trying to scare us, the worst thing we could do is fight amongst ourselves. We have to hold together and face this as a team. My question is, who is doing this? No one outside of this group knows all the detail of our relationships with Dhan. Or at least, I can think of no one."

The silence continued until I became aware of Clark's gaze resting on me. "When I got here yesterday, you were wearing a sweatshirt and jeans. In the evening, you had on one of those Nordic jumpers. When did you change?"

My rage, focused as it was on Simone, took a moment to subside. "I don't know. Just before we had dinner. You were outside, Mika and Simone were finishing the fondue and I was setting the table. I popped upstairs for a minute to get changed. Why?"

"Right. I was collecting wood and Mika was in the kitchen with Simone. The only people upstairs were you and Lovisa. Both of you knew how much money Mika lost ..."

"But only Gael knew that Dhan stole my translation," said Lovisa, her voice soft. "She's the one person who knows what effect it would have to see A+ in the bathroom mirror."

All eyes turned to me. I stared back and for just a second, I questioned myself. Next thing I knew I was on my feet, pointing at them with a shaking finger, my voice just above a whisper.

"You set of judgemental, over-privileged bastards! Of course you'd all suspect me. I'm the one who never quite fitted in. No money, no connections, no class. It may come as a shock to you, but that is exactly why Dhan trusted me above all the rest of you. He was the only person who didn't judge. The truth is that Dhan and I were friends because we actually liked each other. The rest of us have nothing more than a regular guilt trip to bind us."

Clark closed his eyes and shook his head, as if trying to clear it. "Wait, back up there. I have a whole bunch of questions."

"Oh, do you now?" I shouted. "Well, so do I and tonight I want some answers. You don't need to tell me why because I worked out your motives for myself. The missing element is how. What I want to know is how you four worked together to organise the 'accident' that killed Dhan."

If the fire hadn't continued crackling and the music carried on, I would have said that time stopped. Everyone froze, each expression incredulous or shocked or confused.

After a moment, Mika spoke. "Is that why you've been trying to scare us, Gael? To provoke us into some kind of confession because you believe we actively wanted Dhan dead?" He shook his head, his eyes glinting. "After twenty years of spending every other year together, you suspect the rest of us are guilty of murder?" He gave a short cough-laugh, sat back and lifted his face to the ceiling, blinking with wide eyes.

Lovisa opened a hand as if to invite an explanation but Simone drew it back. "Over the years, you have said some horrible, damaging things to me, including this evening. But to accuse us of killing Dhan is completely unforgivable. You have crossed a line, Gael, and you will regret that for the rest of your life."

My head was muddled and I reached for the wine bottle to top up my glass.

Clark withdrew the bottle and pushed a jug of water towards me. "Two things. One. Sober up and stop talking bullshit. Two. You have never been the outsider and I resent you taking that line. Don't you dare try the Irish working-class horseshit. Just don't. Yes, Lovisa, Mika and Simone have always had a sense of

European aristocracy, but let me tell you something. You and Dhan were even worse. British humour, British culture, British innate sense of superiority, you were painfully smug. Trust me, I am familiar with being patronised by my friends and you are guilty of the clique mentality as much as anyone else."

"Clark! Listen, I ..."

"I'm not done. You booked this place, you had access and time the rest of us did not. Look me in the eye, Gael. For whatever reason, are you trying to freak us out?"

I shook my head. "No! None of this weird stuff is down to me, I swear. My theory about twenty years ago is one thing, but even if I wanted answers, I wouldn't try to spook them out of you. My emotions got the better of me tonight, and I apologise for that."

I sat down, hot and confused. Clark passed me the wine bottle and I filled my glass.

After a few moments of silence, Lovisa spoke. "My head tells me to wait for the morning. My heart wants to know now. Do you really, honestly believe we were responsible for Dhan's death? Not in a series of accidents sense, but out of malevolence?"

I rubbed my face with my hands and took another slug of wine. "I don't know. What I can say is that something was very wrong that night. But the reason I don't know is because I wasn't there."

"You weren't there," echoed Simone. "You were lucky. The rest of us must carry a responsibility which haunts me every day of my life. I wake up at night panicking, reliving every single moment and trying to change the story. It never changes and it never will. Gael, drop your conspiracy theory. We didn't kill Dhan. If anything, he killed himself." Her voice cracked a little and Lovisa rested a hand on her shoulder.

We had reached the end of the line. I'd accused my friends of murder, attacked their characters and taken a machete to the bonds of friendship. Perhaps I should just go to bed.

The music player changed from Keane's 'Somewhere Only We Know' to Prince's '1999'. We stared at one another in disbelief and Clark pushed back his chair to deal with the device. He switched it off and in the silence, we heard three loud knocks, the iron ring banging on wood. My skin chilled as we all turned to stare at the front door.

Chapter 23: Gael, now

Seconds passed and no one seemed able to move. Once again, three heavy knocks sounded on the wood, each sending a jolt through my bones. Five of us sat frozen, staring at that huge oak door. Mika got to his feet and jerked his head at Clark. They stood shoulder to shoulder as Mika switched on the outdoor lights and Clark checked the spy hole. We got up from our seats to stand behind them. Clark turned to us, shaking his head with a shrug. Mika threw back the bolts and turned the key. The door creaked open, icy air rushing inwards as we braced ourselves.

Several paces off the porch, out of view of the spy hole, stood a hooded figure, carrying a sack. Unlike the Grim Reaper, this figure was short and rotund, more like a monk or an Ewok. It approached, bowing its head.

A gloved left hand pushed back the cloak to reveal a face we hadn't seen for twenty years.

Dhan.

"Happy New Year, my friends!"

His grin was sheepish as he repeated his eyebrow trick and pulled out a small black lump from his pocket. "If the first person over the threshold is a dark-haired man carrying coal, it's good luck. Can I come in?"

Unconsciously, we all followed the same pattern. Each of us recoiled from something we did not understand. Simone and

Lovisa clutched one another and backed away towards the stairs. Mika reversed as far as the fireplace, shaking his head and making a low hum. Clark and I stood beside the front door, tense and ready to throw this apparition out into the snow.

I was the first to move. My eyes fixed on his; I took one pace after another and reached out a hand. Not to shake or caress, more to prod, as if to check he was flesh and blood. I poked his shoulder and he laughed.

"In my day, it used to be three kisses. Now it's a prod on the shoulder? I've got some cultural assimilation to do, that much is obvious."

We all stared, speechless. It looked like Dhan, albeit twenty years older, with grey temples and flecks of white in his beard. It sounded like Dhan, with all the same cadences of speech.

My mind processed every kind of possibility, real and imagined, in around ninety seconds. Hallucination, twin brother, artificially intelligent replicant, prank played by one of Mika's AI team, nightmare or hologram, but the evidence rebutted me at every attempt to flee reality. After we'd spent twenty years coming to terms with his death, Dhan was not dead.

He was right here in front of us, wearing what looked like a cloak straight out of Star Wars.

Lovisa swept her stare around each of us and settled on the newcomer. "It's gone midnight. Come and join us, stranger."

"Thank you. I brought champagne," said Dhan. "Bottle of top fizz in my Santa sack. I got gifts for all of you. The champagne is chilled because I've been outside for a while, but it's definitely not frozen." He grinned at us like some kind of TV game show host and hoisted his sack onto the coffee table.

The moment shrank away from me, or maybe it was the other way around. I was there, watching Dhan unpack presents from his sack and I was not. I was at a distance, surveying the five statues and the one animated individual who should not have been there.

Lovisa's voice broke the moment. "Mika, could we get another glass?"

As if he were a zombie, Mika obeyed and took another glass from the sideboard, placing it on the table. Dhan – Dhan! – uncorked a bottle of Cristal. Like feral kittens drawn to a saucer of milk, Lovisa, Clark and Simone peeled away from the shadows and stepped nervously closer to the table, Mika's expression hard to read as his back was to the fire.

Lovisa distributed the flutes of fizz, her eyes wide. "I have no idea how to propose a toast," she said. "Tonight was supposed to be an anniversary, a tribute to a friend we had lost. I'm a little confused because out of the blue, he is found."

We stood there, holding glasses, dazed and unable to process current events.

Dhan lifted his glass, his cloak falling to the floor. "To 2020! To our futures! Happy New Year!"

We lifted our flutes and mumbled 'Happy New Year' as if we were programmed. The bubbles slipped down easily and a smile lifted my face. The last twenty years had been a dream. Dhan was alive. Dhan was here, grinning at all of us, knocking his flute against my, Lovisa's, Simone's and Mika's glasses. Only when he got to Clark did he falter.

Clark burst the bubble, snatching his glass away, spilling the contents on his sleeve and snarled. "Happy New Year? Where the fuck have you been for the last twenty?"

Dhan bowed his head and looked up under his eyelashes. From a swell of joy, anger overtook me and right then, I wanted to punch him in the jaw. Twenty years of grief and disruption and he pulls a Lady Diana?

"I know I owe you all an explanation. But before we rake over the past, can we please celebrate the fact we have a future? Come on, Clark, don't let the side down."

Clark didn't move, his champagne glass drawn back towards

his right shoulder.

The impasse was broken by Lovisa. "Let's sit down. There will be many questions and I hope, many answers." The table was set for five, so Mika fetched another chair from the kitchen and set it at the end of the table. Lovisa as Queen, Dhan as King, the rest of us merely courtiers.

The silence dragged on as we sipped our champagne and attempted to formulate the myriad questions we needed to ask. No one seemed keen to go first. We tried not to stare, but time after time I sneaked a glance at this face, this body, this person we had missed so very much.

My mind was in such a state of confusion I could not begin to describe the emotions I felt, and I trusted each of them even less. Time and again, I opened my mouth to speak and reined myself in. Lovisa rested her gaze on Mika's face and I understood. The onus was on him. One more time, he was Dad.

Mika cleared his throat. "Dhan, I would like to say that I'm happy to see you. Perhaps when this evening is over, I will be able to do just that. At this moment, I'm fighting with shock, disbelief, uncertainty and if I'm honest, anger. To paraphrase Clark, where the hell have you been for the last twenty years?"

Dhan nodded, as if in sympathy, but his know-it-all grin spread across his face like a shark's smile. "You lot are bound to have a tonne of questions. I would, in your shoes. I'm going to explain what I did, why I did it and apologise for your troubles. I missed you all, believe me. It's really good to see you again. So, as this is a long story, what are the chances of something to eat?"

No one moved, so I brought another plate from the kitchen. Lovisa and I, apparently the only people who had possession of their motor faculties, pushed the half-eaten curries, dhals and parathas towards him.

He ladled spoon after spoon onto his plate, exclaiming at both quantity and quality. "Been practising your Indian cooking, that much I can see. How cool that you made a banquet tonight with all the …"

I interrupted, my voice tight and furious. "We made an Indian banquet to mark twenty years since your death. Except you're not dead. Now I'm fine with you stuffing your face with our food after wrecking our lives for twenty bloody years, but I think you have some explaining to do."

Dhan held up his hands and hunched his shoulders in a defensive gesture. "OK, fair point. I knew some of you might get freaked out by this. Sorry, I really am."

He didn't look it as he picked up his fork and scooped up some vegetable korma. He ate several mouthfuls, nodding his appreciation and took a swallow of champagne. "Twenty years. Seems crazy long. I wanted to make contact ten years after, but the time wasn't right. I had some weird shit going on."

"So did we," said Clark. "We had spent those years grieving for a lost friend."

Dhan tore off a piece of paratha and dabbed it in his curry. "Oh man, I wish I could have told you. But way back then it was impossible. I had no choice but to disappear." He chewed on his bread and met each pair of eyes around the room, nodding as if that gesture alone could make us understand.

My right leg had begun to tremble and tense, jerking up and down as if it wanted to run away without me. "And how exactly did you disappear? We spent all night, all week, and Mika spent an entire year searching for you. Where did you go?"

In my peripheral vision, I saw Clark turn to his left, watching Simone. He removed the champagne glass from her clenched fist and set it on the table. He placed his right hand around her claw and pressed his uninjured shoulder against hers. It was a good move. The pressure building inside that woman was volcanic. Her eyes burned black as pig iron in the furnace.

I looked to Lovisa, who met my eyes with a fearful uncertainty. Simone's attention was 100% on Dhan. She stared at him, her nostrils flaring as if she were a young racehorse about to bolt. The tension in the room cranked up to a low hum and I sensed we only had minutes before someone popped their cork.

Dhan was still eating. "Twenty years ago, our man, is not really the right place to start if we want to tell the story right."

A fist smashed onto the table, startling everyone, shaking glasses and wobbling crockery. I was surprised to see that fist was Mika's. He hissed through his teeth. "Dhan! What happened that night?"

He put down his fork and looked around the table, meeting each pair of eyes with an attempt at regret and sincerity. "I've tried so many times in my head to explain this to you all. More than anything in the world, I want you to understand why I did what I did. You need to know that I suffered immense regret over what I put you through. Until I faced you in person and gave you an explanation, I knew I would never feel at peace. That is why I came here tonight. New decade, new slate. I've missed you guys."

Clark and Simone, clenched together like siblings at a graveside, stared at him with a cold incomprehension. Mika pressed his fingers to the bridge of his nose, flicking his gaze from tablecloth to Dhan to tablecloth again. Lovisa was massaging her own temples, her eyes closed.

I inhaled a long calming breath and allowed my shoulders to drop on the exhale. I fixed Dhan with an intense stare and repeated, "What happened?"

"What happened? I can give you the 'what', that's easy. The 'why' might take longer. The short story is I jumped in the lake, dived under the ice and swam to the jetty. I got out and wrapped myself in heat blankets, then crept away to hide in the laundry room. I stayed there for a couple of hours, until I had dried off and warmed up. When the police quit for the night, I got dressed in full ski gear and walked parallel to the lane through the forest until I reached the main road. That was where I hitched a lift to Prague and yeah, well, went underground."

Mika's head swung from side to side, each sinew in his neck creaking like a tree trunk. "That is impossible. You could never have swum out of the lake. In those temperatures? Even if you had managed to get out, you'd have frozen to death. It was -11°! Look at who you're talking to. That was my lake!"

Dhan spread his palms and shrugged once again. He didn't need to say a word. He was here, in the flesh, right in front of everyone's eyes.

"You arrogant arsehole," spat Clark. "You actually sit there patting yourself on the back for faking your own death? You have no clue what impact that had on the rest of us. How dare you walk in here and say sorry for inflicting twenty years of grief on your friends?"

Mika's stare began to unnerve me. He didn't take his eyes off Dhan. Opposite me came the slight puffing sound of Simone suppressing tears. Lovisa put an arm around her shoulders and drew her close. I noticed Dhan couldn't meet Mika's eyes. For several minutes no one spoke. The fire was getting low but to leave my place at that table was unthinkable. All I could manage was to identify wave after wave of intense emotion. Fury, confusion, sympathy, disbelief, exasperation, weariness, and one more time and enraged resentment at twenty wasted years.

"Your family, your friends ... why?" I stopped, unable to trust my voice. I took several huge breaths, swallowing to release the constriction in my throat. I would not cry. If Simone could manage not to weep, then so could I.

Dhan pushed his plate away. "My family, my friends were part of the reason why. That's the hard bit to explain. I'm going to try, with you guys at least. The day after tomorrow, I'm travelling back to Britain. I've already accepted that I will never make my family understand, so I'm going to tell them I had amnesia. There's no way they will ever understand the truth."

Lovisa's voice was soft. "Your mother and father worshipped you. Their son was their sun and their moon. You broke their hearts. How could you? How can you reappear after twenty years and make up for all that time?"

Dhan shook his head, his expression sorrowful. "My dad died six months ago and my mother only lasted two months without him. All that's left now are my sisters and the distribution of the family business. That's one of the many reasons I needed to come out of the shadows."

Not one of us spoke, processing the implications of what he had just said.

Dhan looked around the table, at each face in turn. "What I want you to understand is that in my early twenties I screwed everything up. Nothing had gone the way I wanted. It wasn't supposed to happen like that. To my mind, I had to start again and not make so many mistakes this time. My life had got ... entangled and I couldn't see a way out. In the end, I made up my mind to just disappear. It was a drastic solution, I know, but the only route to a clean break. The lake gave me the perfect opportunity and I took it."

"What do you mean by 'entangled'?" Lovisa's voice was steady and neutral but I knew her too well. I recognised that chilly sliver hinting at the iceberg beneath.

Dhan wagged his head from side to side, an evasive gesture. "Everyone wanted something from me and I couldn't deliver. Simone was pregnant ..."

"You knew?" Simone's mouth dropped open.

"I suspected. The thing is, I couldn't become a father. No way was I responsible enough for myself, leave alone any dependants. Not only that, but my parents had promised me as the groom to another family's daughter. It was all arranged." He shot a quick glance at me. I continued staring at him, expressionless.

"So that was one problem. Another was that I owed Mika an explanation. The new business I'd asked you to fund had already folded and the money was gone. I just didn't know how to tell you," he said. "It was completely my fault."

"You owed me more than an explanation," said Mika. "You owed me thirty thousand Euros." His flat delivery showed how tightly he was holding on to his temper.

"Which I didn't have. But you've done OK out of the idea, right? I keep an eye on your company and it's flying, mate." He grinned at Mika who didn't move a single muscle in his face.

"As for Clark, I messed up there, buddy. I knew you had feelings for me and I gave you the wrong idea. That wasn't fair. Not fair at all."

"Don't patronise me, you shit." Clark's eyes were nothing more than slits and the muscles of his forearm flexed as he clenched his fists.

"Not meant as patronising in any way. Just owning up to my mistakes." He turned to Lovisa and I recognised his modus operandi. He was looking for an ally, hoping to get just one of us on side. The heat of my anger subsided into a cool observation. After twenty years, Dhan hadn't changed at all. Even now, he still thought his charm and claims to loyalty would win the day. Everything he had said was to justify himself. I stood up and placed another couple of logs on the fire, as if what was happening was completely normal. Then I returned to the table to watch Dhan attempt to exonerate himself in the eyes of Lovisa.

"Yes?" Lovisa asked. "Come on, I'm intrigued. In what way did your plagiarism of my work 'entangle' you? Perhaps you were under pressure to maintain the grade standard you stole from me? How awfully unfortunate that must have been." Her words came out painfully, as if through broken glass.

"Lovisa, you know it wasn't like that. I did copy your paper and I admitted it and apologised, yeah? My situation was desperate and I needed a favour. I told you in Prague I saw it as borrowing, not stealing. You had more than enough in terms of credits and high grades, so you could afford to drop a semester.

I checked the university website on graduation day. You sailed through your finals with a distinction. At the end of the day, no harm done."

Everyone's attention was focused on Lovisa at one end of the table, watching for her reaction, so none of them saw my move coming. To be honest, I took myself by surprise. The first thing I knew was Dhan on his feet, stumbling backwards, brushing champagne out of his eyes and I held an empty glass in my right hand.

"No harm done? No harm done!" My voice was raw, as if I'd been screaming. "You selfish bastard!" I snatched up Dhan's own glass of champagne and flung the contents at his face.

He ducked sideways and the champagne sailed past him onto the rug. "Gael, stop it! Let me explain, will you?"

"No! I'm not listening to any more of this. You swan in here with your explanations and excuses without a moment's thought for what we suffered. And the last few days? With your stupid shitty pranks to let us know you were back. You idiot! You stupid inconsiderate imbecile! After twenty years of grieving, you turn up to scare us, hurt us and fracture those rare moments of peace we can enjoy together. I could kill you. Right now, with my bare hands, I could kill you!"

By then, everyone was on their feet. The raging electricity I emanated clearly scared the whole room, but only Clark was brave enough to put a reassuring hand on my shoulder.

His eyes on me, Dhan stepped away from me and picked up a napkin to wipe his face. "OK, maybe some of those weren't my greatest ideas. I didn't want to hurt anyone. The stuff with the car – letting down the tyre and that monster snowball – were designed to tip a wink to your driving skills. But I mistimed both. Sorry about your shoulder, Clark."

Lovisa held up her bandaged hand.

"What did you do? And how is that my fault?" Dhan asked, with a touch of belligerence.

"Picking up glass from a shattered bottle of Moët et Chandon."

"Oh, hell. That wasn't supposed to happen. Look, you guys, I just wanted to share a few in-jokes, remind you of some of the laughs we had, so that when I turned up on the doorstep, it wouldn't be such a shock. My bad."

Simone's face was grey as chalk. "In-jokes? You put a child's ski suit upstairs on the hook after I aborted our baby. What kind of sick mind could perceive that as funny?"

Clark and Mika regarded Dhan with such an expression of disgust it would have sent me running out into the snow, never to come back.

"No! Jeez, Simone, that was *not* for you. All I did for you was the French maid pinafore. The ski suit was a joke for Lovisa. When we used to go skiing in Geneva, she always told me I could go to the nursery slopes with the other toddlers. That's why I put that little suit there, as if I was back from the nursery slopes. As if I would do something so crass. I'm so sorry, it never crossed my mind you would see that as a reference to …"

"A dead child." Simone's expression had as much animation as that of a rattlesnake.

We were all standing, breathing heavily as if we'd been running. Resentment fuelled by shock and alcohol combined to create a poisonous atmosphere.

Mika spoke, forever the adult in the room. "It's late, or perhaps I should say early. We've all had a lot to drink and even more to take in. I suggest we leave the conversation here and get some sleep. After a decent rest, I think we'll all be better prepared to get our heads around what has happened. Let's leave the table as it is and clean up in the morning. Dhan, where are you staying? I assume you have somewhere nearby?"

He was still dabbing water from his hair and stubbly beard. "I rented a campervan, so I could move around. Tonight, I parked it down the road, in the forest and walked here. Thing is, it's pretty cold in there at night. Would anyone mind if I crashed on the sofa? Or if there was a spare room…"

Without a word, Simone pushed back her chair with such violence it fell over, walked away from the table and up the stairs. Lovisa followed, throwing a glance at me.

Clark met Mika's eyes, his expression mutinous. "I think we should kick the lying bastard out into the snow, but I'll leave the decision up to you. One thing, Mika, if he stays, he stays on the sofa. I don't want him upstairs with us. Period. See you in the morning."

Once Clark had gone, Mika checked the front door and pulled the guard across the fire. I found a couple of throws for Dhan to use as a bed cover. Pungent wafts left over from our banquet permeated the room, so I began to clear the table.

Dhan waved a hand at me as if I were a servant. "Leave that, mate. I can sort it out. Thank you for letting me stay. Hopefully, in the morning, they'll find it easier to understand why I did what I did. Goodnight, Mika, goodnight Gael."

I nodded once and turned to climb the stairs, Mika on my heels. Once I reached the first floor, I saw the door to Simone's room was open and dark. Lovisa's was shut and a strip of light showed from beneath her door. Mika faced me and bent to press his forehead against mine.

"Goodnight, Gael."

"Night, Mika."

In the bathroom, I washed my face and cleaned my teeth. On tiptoe, I crept past Lovisa's room. No more drama or discussions till morning, I was wrung out. A pop from downstairs stopped me in my tracks. I padded halfway down the steps to peer into the living room.

Dhan was sitting at the dining table, pouring himself a glass of champagne from a fresh bottle he'd taken from our fridge. He gathered all the dishes of leftovers towards him and as I watched from the shadows, he began to eat.

Moving like a ghost, I went to knock on Lovisa's door.

Chapter 24: Gael, now

The three of us sat in Lovisa's room for over an hour, comforting, crying and whispering to each other. Finally, Simone and I chose to wash our puffy faces and rest in our own beds. We exhorted each other to lock our doors. I lay on the bed, fully clothed, telling myself I would get up in a moment, undress and switch off my mind. I didn't. Instead, I stared at the snowflakes falling past my window, playing over and over scenes from the previous twenty years. The endless police station interviews, the awful memorial service, that lunch we shared with Dhan's devastated family, ten different New Year's Eves paying tribute to a man who wasn't dead. Grief, guilt, loss, decades of pain all for nothing.

The house creaked and gurgled, and every groan of timber alerted my system like a jolt of electricity. My eyes were scratchy and dry but I couldn't seem to lift my head off the pillow. I catnapped, having strange half dreams in which the wind whisked away my beach ball and blew it out to sea. When I ran after it, a sleek grey shape rose from the waves, caught the ball and took it underwater. It was a seal and it was also Dhan. My dream self cried hot, hiccupping, childish tears.

A sound woke me. This time it was not the snaps or shifts of an old wooden building. Someone was outside my door. The tapping came again, accompanied by a faint whisper.

"Gael? Gael are you awake?"

I sat up and stared at the door. The voice came again.

"Gael, it's Clark. I need your help."

I scrambled to my feet and unlocked the door. Clark stood there, fully dressed apart from his sling. He looked over his shoulder and slipped inside the room. He locked the door and rested his back against it.

"Sorry to wake you." He took in what I was wearing. "You not been to bed either?"

I rubbed my eyes. "Not really. Dozed a bit but had some really weird dreams. Why do you need my help?"

"Painkillers, please. The alcohol has worn off and my shoulder hurts like a bastard. Do you have any more of those pills you gave me?"

"They weren't mine, they were Lovisa's. Go in the bathroom across the landing and there is a first-aid box on the cabinet. She's got plenty in there." I sat back on the bed, resting my forearms on my knees. Rather than leaving the room to search for his drugs, Clark sat next to me, wrapping his right arm around my shoulders and pulling me towards his chest. I rested my head against his chin and took in the scent of the man. Wherever we were, island, city, mountain or beach, Clark smelled of pine forest. We sat like that for several minutes, taking comfort in each other's presence. The reassurance was soporific.

"Listen," he whispered. "None of us can handle this freak show if we spend all night awake. I'm gonna pop some pills and you should slug one of these. Kinda like cocoa with a kick."

He pulled out a miniature bottle from his pocket. Bailey's Irish Cream. I laughed and shook my head. "You know me, Clark, never been interested in the sweet stuff."

"Who gives a goddamn about the taste? Drink it, down in one, and get some decent rest. Trust me, this is exactly what you need." He twisted the cap from the bottle and handed it to me.

I passed the bottle under my nose and the tempting hint of

whiskey promising a silky caress overpowered my resistance. I drank it, in three mouthfuls. Clark took the bottle from my hand, eased me gently back on the bed and covered me with the duvet.

His lips, dry and soft, met my forehead, with a little pressure. "Sleep tight, sweetcheeks. Tomorrow's another decade." His weight left the mattress and the door closed.

When I awoke, sweaty with a thumping head, desert-dry mouth and itchy eyes, my number one priority was to get to the bathroom. Outside, it was not quite light. The sky had a bluish tinge preceding dawn but I was not in the mood to admire the sunrise. All my focus was upon my bodily needs. I threw back the duvet, grimacing as the equilibrium in my head adjusted. I placed my feet on the floor and with the assistance of the bedside table, managed to stand and turn on the light. My eyes squeezed shut in the glare. Hellfire, how much had I drunk? In my memory, almost nothing. I threw most of it over Dhan.

Dhan.

The memory of last night hit me like a bucket of cold water in the face. I stood there, willing my head to clear until my bladder insisted I move. I tugged at the door handle but it held fast. Of course, we all locked our doors when we went to bed. I blinked. There was no key. I looked around the room, wondering where on earth I would have put the key. The bladder situation became an emergency. I tugged at the door handle, kicked at the door, shouted for Lovisa or Simone to help me, but there was no reply. Panic seized me and I searched the room for some kind of vessel in which I could pee. The plastic waste paper bin caught my eye. I hauled out the plastic liner and squatted over the bin, a blessed release. As my sense of panic subsided, my puzzlement grew. Why was my bedroom door locked? Where was the key? Where was everyone else? What time was it?

I cleaned up and parked the bin in the corner, covering it with a T-shirt, then searched the whole room for the key. Drunk and emotional, I must have locked the door and taken out the key for safe-keeping. Under my pillow? On the dressing-table? There was a half-drunk bottle of water on the windowsill which I grabbed and glugged, thankful to myself for leaving it there. The act of tipping the bottle to my lips triggered a memory.

Clark was here. Sometime in the night, Clark came in and gave me a mini bottle of Bailey's Irish Cream. No wonder my head was so muggy. I never drank whiskey in any form. But if Clark was in my room, how come it was now locked? I sat on my bed, trying to process events. Then I pulled back the curtains and stared out at the featureless greyscape, seeing nothing but endlessly falling snow. Crouching by the door, I squinted through the keyhole. No light, no keyhole view of the landing, nothing. Which leads a logical mind to deduce that there is a key in the keyhole. On the outside.

I sat back on my bottom, cross-legged, trying to work out why I was locked in my room. I pressed my ear to the door and listened for any sign of life. Nothing. Any kid who grew up with sneaky siblings knows one trick you can try with a locked door. There was enough of a gap between floor and door to roll a cigar through. A few seconds rummaging through my belongings and I found a printout of all the terms and conditions of the chalet. I slid it under the door and positioned it right underneath the door handle and keyhole. Then I grabbed my make-up bag and selected a pair of tweezers. I sat as close as I could get to the door, inserted the tweezers into the keyhole and pinched the end of the key. I twisted right, left, right a bit further and when the mechanics settled into place with my pincers pressed either side of the key, I pushed backwards. The key moved, as I hoped it would, but the big wooden door was wider than my weedy tweezers. I pressed and pushed as far as it would go, but the key remained loosely in the lock.

Breathe. I took three huge breaths to calm my mind, and visualised the lock. The key was probably less than a third into the lock. In the correct position, with the correct tool, I could push it back until it fell onto the paper and I could draw it under the door. The tweezers were too short. There had to be something in this room or in my luggage that I could use to eject the key. I closed my eyes and concentrated on exactly the type of thing I needed and trusted my mind to deliver the answer. Unbidden, Dhan's eyebrows appeared in my mind. I opened my eyes. Eyebrows. I went back to my make-up bag and found my eyebrow brush. Long, thin and with a comb and brush end, it was perfect for eyebrows and eyelashes and now, keyholes.

Twenty seconds later, the key slipped out of the lock and thudded onto the paper. I drew it carefully under the door and into the room with a childlike sense of triumph. *Gotcha!* I unlocked the door and stepped out onto the landing. Every other door on this floor was open and from where I stood, I could see they were all empty. I took my ersatz potty into the bathroom and emptied it into the toilet. While washing and cleaning the bin, the urge to do the same for myself became overpowering. I stripped off the clothes I'd worn all night and jumped into the shower, making sure to lock the bathroom door.

Washed, dressed and feeling a lot better than I had when I woke up, I made my wary way downstairs. The clock said 06.45 and the place was empty. On the sofa was a bundle of bedclothes, but no trace of our unexpected guest. All the plates and serving dishes from last night were still on the dining table, stinking of curry. I started clearing the table because the smell was making me feel sick. Once I'd switched on the dishwasher and washed all the pans, I went upstairs to the top floor to see if the guys were still in bed. Both Clark's and Mika's rooms were empty, as was their bathroom. The fourth door on that floor was closed. Had Dhan got uncomfortable on the sofa and come up to sleep here? I tapped on the door. No answer. With some trepidation, I turned the handle and eased it open. Inside, a neatly made bed which had not been slept in. I closed the door and checked the rack beside the back door. All their ski suits were still there, including the child's one Simone had mentioned last night. So where had they gone and why did they lock me into my room?

My stomach gave a long whining sound, like a cat yawning. I descended to the kitchen and made myself some coffee and French toast. The food helped clear my head and settle my stomach. The final touch would be to get some fresh air. I looked out of the window at the snow. Not the crisp sunny day I could have hoped for, and in this low cloud, visibility would be poor. But I wouldn't go far. Perhaps just a short stroll down the lane and back.

I returned to my room for a jumper and some thick socks. Out of the window, I saw people approaching along the ski trail, one dragging a sled. As they drew closer, I recognised Mika. His height always gave him away. I ran up the flight of stairs to greet them as they arrived at the back door.

Simone was unlocking the door and stopped short when she saw me bounding up the last few steps. I couldn't hear what she said to the others, but they all stared at me as if in shock. Lovisa was the first to enter.

"Good morning, Gael, and happy New Year!" She held out her arms for a hug and I pressed my warm cheeks against a freezing face. "How did you sleep?"

"Happy New Year to you too! Where have you been?"

The other three bundled into the room after knocking the snow from their boots. I saw no sign of the sledge. We wished each other Happy New Year and I hugged each of them in turn. As they unzipped, and laced and unbuckled their outdoor things, I couldn't wait to ask my questions.

"So? Where have you been? When I woke up, my bedroom door was locked from the outside. Which of you did that, and why? And where did Dhan go?"

Lovisa pulled off her glove with a wince, and I saw the bandage beneath was bloody. Simone was assisting Clark in taking off his jacket.

Mika shook his head, but kept his gaze averted. "We don't know where he is. That's where we've been, out looking for him. When we came down this morning, he was gone."

"What? When?" I demanded, trying to meet any pair of eyes.

"Gael, my mistake," said Clark. "I locked your bedroom door as I left last night because you were fast asleep. I meant to push the key under the door but I got distracted. Sorry, I'm an idiot." He put his sling back on.

Something was very wrong. Clark's face was white and bloodless, his lips the blue-grey colour of a vein. The air held a charge, as if all the things unsaid hung over us like a wet veil.

Lovisa reached out and touched my arm. "Could you give me a hand changing this bandage, Gael? Maybe I should have applied butterfly stitches, the cut was rather deep. Let's go downstairs to our bathroom and then we should make some coffee. We need to warm up and talk about what happened last night."

She guided me downstairs and took me straight into our bathroom. I crouched in front of her as she sat on the toilet seat. She didn't utter a murmur while I unwound the bloody bandage, cleaned the wound across her palm and applied antiseptic cream and a new dressing.

"What did you do, Lovisa?"

Our eyes met and she gave me a weak smile. "Nothing. We'll try again later. Thank you for this. Now unless I get some caffeine in my system in the next five minutes, I'm liable to fall asleep in the bath."

We went down to the living room, where Mika and Simone were cleaning.

"Oh, you are a pair of angels!" Lovisa exclaimed.

"Not really. Gael had already done most of it. Cleared the

table and put everything in the dishwasher. She's the angel," Simone smiled.

"No problem. The smell of yesterday's food was pretty nauseating first thing this morning."

"Well, thank you anyway. We shouldn't have left that to you. Who wants what for coffee? I need a triple espresso."

"Latte for me," Simone trilled, unusually brittle even for her. "Just finishing up here. You know how I hate leaving the place in a mess." She took the washing along to the little utility room beside the sauna. I really couldn't see the point. She might as well leave it with the rest of our dirty bed linen. But I didn't argue. With Simone there's very little point.

"Mika? Latte OK for you too?" Lovisa asked, her voice tentative.

"Sure. Why don't you two close the kitchen door? I'm going to run the vacuum cleaner through here. Our banquet made a real mess."

I closed the door and turned to face Lovisa, folding my arms. "Right, what is going on? Everyone is behaving very weirdly. Why were you up so early? Where have you been? Where the hell is Dhan? Don't treat me like a child, Lovisa. I'm a bloody journalist and all my instincts for a story tell me something here doesn't fit. What happened?"

She busied herself with a pan of milk and filled the reservoir of the coffee machine with fresh water. "Yes, things are very weird. The problem is, I don't think anyone knows exactly what happened. Let's wait till we are all here and piece together events by sharing our experiences, OK? Why don't you slice bread and get some cheese and ham out of the fridge. I expect everyone is hungry. It's such a shame about the weather. I had planned a long hike for us all along the next mountain. So frustrating when you can see no further than three metres ahead of your face."

I recognised Lovisa-style dissembling when I heard it. So I shut up, sliced the bread, arranged our usual breakfast assortment in the middle of the table – cheese, ham, jam, plus peanut butter for Clark and Marmite for me – and waited for the others to join us.

The door opened and Simone came in, with a bright smile. Too bright. "There, living room restored to normal. Mmm, this looks good. Is there any orange juice?"

I poured her a glass and one for myself. Mika joined us and sat silently at the table, leaning on his forearms. Lovisa handed him a coffee and he took it. Muscles in his jaw twitched and pulsed, but he kept his eyes on the table, apparently fascinated by a pot of raspberry jam. By the time Lovisa had served all of us, Clark came into the room, his eyes hollow.

"Jeez. And I thought I had a high pain threshold. I took another two just now and borrowed four more for the journey home. I'll replace them, Lovisa, I promise."

"Don't be ridiculous. I can get these at cost price. You take as many as you need. Maybe we should eat some breakfast now and talk about last night." Her eyes flicked to Mika but he shook his head. "Clark, you said you couldn't sleep?"

"Right." Clark slathered peanut butter and raspberry jam over a slice of bread with his free hand. "Gael gave me some pills yesterday morning, so when the alcohol wasn't cutting it at around four in the morning, I knocked on her door and asked for more, correct?"

"Yes, and I told you they were Lovisa's and you could find them in the bathroom. Then you gave me some Bailey's to help me sleep." A thought occurred to me. "Where did you get it from? Do you always carry miniature bottles of alcohol to comfort damsels in distress?"

No one cracked a smile.

"I dunno. I find the most random things in my suitcase. Thought I'd offer it to you as a trade for the painkillers. I tucked you up in bed and remembered to lock your door. The plan was to push the key underneath so you could get out when you woke up. But while I was locking the door, I heard noises from downstairs."

Mika jerked as if he'd been hit with a cattle prod. "Yes! Noises. Clark came to wake me although I wasn't asleep. Neither of us wanted to go downstairs alone, so we went together to investigate. The front door was wide open and there was no one on the sofa. His coat, his sack, everything had gone. We went outside to look around but in that weather, we couldn't see a thing. So we came inside to put on winter clothes and find a torch."

I studied Mika's expression. The man looked wrecked, haunted. I reached across the table to clasp his hand and he flinched.

"Sorry, I'm a bit jumpy. Low blood sugar. I need to eat something. Simone, will you pass me some cheese?"

Simone did so; Mika put a slice on a piece of bread and then sat there staring at it.

"I couldn't sleep either," said Simone. "I put on my bedside lamp and tried to write down my feelings in my journal. Mika and Clark saw the light, knocked on my door and told me they were going to look for Dhan. I got up to join them and Lovisa heard us whispering."

This was the most ridiculous badly rehearsed script I'd ever heard.

"Eat, Mika," exhorted Lovisa. "We all need to eat. Yes, four of us were awake and worried that Dhan had walked off into the snow. We got dressed in outdoor gear and went looking for him. We walked down the lane to where he said he parked his van and found nothing. We came back along the ski tracks just in case he went that way. He has gone. Just gone. It's been snowing all night so there are no tracks, no footprints, no way of knowing where he went."

I puffed air from the corner of my mouth. "You should have woken me; I would have come with you. OK, so here's what I think. Dhan didn't feel he got the reception he expected and left in the middle of the night. We can drive down to the village. He probably parked up there to get some food. He can't be too far away. Find van, find Dhan. Where else is he likely to go?"

Clark stirred his coffee, Simone drank her juice, and Lovisa buttered a piece of bread. Mika sat still as a lump of granite.

"What?" I demanded. "What is wrong with you all?"

Lovisa rubbed her temples. "What's wrong with us all is probably the same thing. Emotionally overwrought, little to no sleep and all of us trying to process the shock of last night. I don't know about any of you, but in one evening my whole belief system has changed."

Mika picked up his bread and cheese and took a huge bite. We waited till he had swallowed and was ready to speak. "Gael is right. We should take the hire car down the lane to see if we can find Dhan's van. Clark and I will do that, right after breakfast. We need to find that van."

"We need to find that man," I said, unscrewing the jar of Marmite. "This feels like some kind of bizarre dream."

Everyone nodded, staring at the table. We ate in silence, the atmosphere buzzing with unspoken thoughts.

Eventually, I remembered I had a question. "Why did you take the sledge?"

Simone looked at me, her eyes wide. "Sorry? What do you mean?"

I had the strangest sense that everyone was holding their breath. "I saw you coming back. I was in my room, getting ready to go out for a walk and you all emerged out of the snow along the ski trail. Four of you in your winter coats, Mika pulling a sledge. If you went out looking for Dhan, what reason would you have to take the sledge?"

"Oh, that was Lovisa's idea," said Simone, speaking in her fast, breathy style. "She pointed out that if Dhan had fallen in the snow or hurt himself, we'd need something to help us carry him.

You know what, I'm still hungry. Anyone else fancy a boiled egg?"

"Good idea," said Lovisa. "Yes, please."

"Not for me, thanks," said Clark, getting to his feet. "Mika, shall we go look for Dhan's vehicle? Then maybe you could take me into the town so I can catch a train. Sorry, guys, but as I said last night, I'm going to cut this trip short, get home and seek medical attention."

"Sure. I understand." Mika stood up and finished his coffee.

To my amazement, neither Simone nor Lovisa protested.

"Clark!" I said. "You can't leave us now. Surely you want to speak to Dhan as much as the rest of us. I get the fact your arm hurts, but we need to work this out together. Please don't go."

He gave me a fond smile. "Sorry, you guys, but I'm outta here. Listen, what say I take the Eurostar and come visit you in Brussels when I'm better? Never been to Brussels before."

"You can come to Brussels whenever you like, but I really can't understand why you'd leave us now. We have so much to talk about, so much to ask Dhan. I want some answers. Don't you?"

Clark wagged his head from side to side, not a yes, not a no. The gesture reminded me of Dhan, which whipped up a strange storm of emotion I couldn't control. I gave in.

"All right, if you have to go, I'll come along for the ride to see you off."

"No!" Mika and Clark spoke as one. Mika's eyes bored into Lovisa's and he looked as if he were about to cry.

"Why not?" I demanded.

Lovisa leaned towards me. "Gael, I'd prefer it if you stayed here. Last night, talking things through with you and Simone cleared my head. But this morning, I feel back to square one. Let Mika and Clark see if they can find Dhan's camper van while the three of us stay here and have a frank conversation. I don't know about you, but I have a cauldron of conflicting emotions I could use some help in processing."

The water Simone had put on for the eggs was boiling madly, splashing onto the hob. The noise caught my attention and I saw she was just standing there, an egg in each hand, staring at me.

"What *is* the matter with you people this morning?" I asked.

Clark came round the table and held his right arm out for a hug. I stood to embrace him.

"We are all freaked. Each of us has gotta deal with this in our own way. See you in Brussels, yeah? Love you, sweetcheeks."

I breathed in, uneasy and discomfited by the fact everyone seemed to be treating me with kid gloves. Clark said his goodbyes to each of us and we followed him out to the living room, where I was surprised to see his case already packed and standing by the front door. The three of us watched from the porch as they drove away, Clark's right hand waving out of the passenger window. His departure seemed cruel and sudden, and I was aware tears were seeping from my eyes. We should have stayed together. Our stability depended on all five of us. Simone linked her arm through the crook of my elbow and ushered me indoors.

That was the moment I stopped asking questions.

Chapter 25: Clark, Two Years Later

I never made it to Brussels. Gael and I talked about it a couple of times, but we both knew it was never going to happen. I had no desire to see any of them again. What was the point? I keep up with the others via social media or news, but I avoided meeting up in person even before the whole virus lockdown. I don't plan on attending another reunion. Ever. Not that anyone suggested we meet for New Year's this time.

When we moved away, I changed my email address and didn't tell them. Best of all, I don't need to explain myself. As a new father, it's natural I want to be with my wife and baby daughter. I'm a different person now, in a constant state of wonder at this tiny human being we made. I want to keep things perfect for her, and that means letting go of the world as it used to be.

This was our first Christmas outside Europe and it was weird, but in a good way. Although I had mixed feelings about leaving after a quarter of a century, my priorities have changed. Jen is pregnant again. We're going to be a family of four and I want us to live somewhere that feels permanent. My life has always been about moving forward. New places, new experiences, new friends, new countries, new cultures, new adventures and no looking back. Right now, I don't want to live in the US and Jen was desperate to get away from the UK. So we compromised. Nova Scotia, Canada has become our new home.

Jen can teach, I can manage all my clients' funds by working from home and arrange my lifestyle around being a stay-at-home dad. I'm looking forward, not back. Just the four of us, by the sea, breathing the ocean air and growing older together.

Europe gave me a lot, including many happy memories and unforgettable experiences. But it also left me with some horrible nightmares. I mean horrible, the kind where you wake up gasping and screaming. In these night terrors, I'm awake and asleep at the same time. I can see some kind of danger creeping up on me or my family. It might be a spider crawling towards my open mouth or a guy with an axe climbing through my daughter's bedroom window. Awake Me is trying to scream but Asleep Me can't open my mouth. Apparently, I make some terrible howling noises until Jen manages to rouse me. Those kind of dreams don't happen often, but when they do, it's impossible to go back to sleep. So I get up and go for a run. Anything rather than lie there in the small hours, thinking.

Jen suggested hypnotherapy. No thanks. As I said, better never to look back.

When the temperatures drop, my shoulder still hurts.

Chapter 26: Simone, Two Years Later

The first time we went to America, my friends teased me about my reactions to New York. Mika in particular was quite cutting. What they didn't understand is that I was trained in the right way of doing things. People laugh at finishing school as if it is filled with silly debutantes. What they do not comprehend is that these places teach one how to behave in a stratum of society inaccessible to most. Gaining mastery over your baser urges is essential, whether that is eating, reading trashy magazines, refusing to exercise and yes, putting a slice of blue cheese on a breakfast pastry. They teach us restraint. Something people like Clark and Gael would never learn.

In my position, one learns to be an actor, playing the role of society wife, hostess, patron of the arts and charming guest. One learns the value of self-control and how to reinvent oneself. If we have learned anything since the health and economic catastrophes of last year, it is how to defer our gratification. There is not much to thank 2020 for, but I am grateful for that.

The university reunions have come to an abrupt halt, understandably. There is nothing left to say to each other. In fact, I have lost touch with many friends since my wedding, largely because I am so busy. For the passing of this year, my husband

and I will be in New York, attending a ball thrown by one of his clients. From there, we will travel to Mexico for a winter break. Vincent prefers swimming, heat and sunshine to skiing, snow and chalets. Personally, I could not agree more. We are perfectly suited to one another.

Lovisa came home from Africa over Christmas. My schedule was so full; I had no time for a lunch or even a coffee. Instead, we invited her for dinner *chez nous* on St Stephen's Day. Vincent knows reams of eligible men, so balancing the table was easy. The evening was a triumph, especially the menu created by our new chef. Unfortunately there was not much opportunity for conversation as I had fifteen other guests to attend to, and Lovisa left early. Two days later, she sent a warm thank you. It was only by email, not card, but the sentiments seemed heartfelt. Vincent and I agreed it was a marvellous thing she was doing and we should think about donating to her charity. Despite all that sun on fair skin, she looked well.

Chapter 27: Lovisa, Two Years Later

Today, I took another tough decision. Two of the children must be isolated from their peers because they have high temperatures and a cough. It was a heart-breaking moment, as Shemu and Asuwema don't understand why they are locked away from their friends. They're too young to remember the previous pandemic. Even the adults' recollections have faded. But as the familiar symptoms presented themselves, a sliver of ice slid down my spine. *Please no, not again.*

I took them out of class myself and instructed the teacher to send the other children out for extra playtime and disinfect her room. The heat and sunshine will add a thin layer of protection, for the kids if not the teacher. The most likely explanation is that it's a mild dose of flu and they'll both recover fast. However, with 140 children under my care, I can't take the risk of anything spreading.

There's a level of guilt about even the best case scenario. I travelled to Europe for a week over Christmas. If it is common influenza, the culprit who transmitted the bug is almost certainly me. If it's something worse ... I'd rather not think about it. I'm not sure I'm strong enough to go through all that again.

The irony of it! I didn't want to go back to Switzerland,

loathed the whole experience and saw hardly any of my friends. Geneva was cold, bleak and like any other European city at Christmas, obsessed with overindulgence. It made me absolutely nauseous and as always, I live in fear sudden restrictions will mean I cannot get back where I'm most needed.

I had dinner at Simone's house with a bunch of awful, self-interested bores and found her husband actually chilling. What she calls his 'sense of humour' is anything but funny. He's callous, cynical, and I rarely say this about anyone, but he has evil in his heart. No one even attempted to organise the New Year's Eve party, but just to give myself an excuse, I booked a flight out on 30 December. I do still love my friends but could only cope with one at a time after what happened.

Gael refused my invitation to spend a day together, saying she was reducing her carbon footprint. We talked on the phone instead but I can sense her resentment. There's nothing I can say, no explanation she would accept.

I spoke to Shemu and Asuwema this evening, in their separate rooms of course. I told them both that sometimes, being excluded from a situation is for a good reason. In some cases, their sacrifice saves the rest. In others, they are spared from circumstances they do not deserve. I blew each a kiss, told them to sleep and locked the door till the morning.

Chapter 28: Mika, Two Years Later

On my computer, I use a master password. You can't write it down or record it anywhere, because if you get hacked, access to your emails, bank accounts, work sites and even your grocery shopping is open to all. My password is committed to memory. It saves me typing in my ID for all the platforms and apps I use.

The remote socialising app we developed two years ago was the single thing that got my company through the crisis. People still want to connect especially when they are forced to keep their distance. Even when the restrictions were lifted, the app remained popular.

We're not having a university reunion this year, remotely or in person. Thank God. Just the thought of trying to avoid the elephant in the room is unbearable. I doubt I'll ever see them again.

Clark is playing happy families in Canada and good luck to him. He fled to the furthest point he could find to quash any suggestion of visitors. Not that any of us would try. After all, he was the first to run.

Lovisa sent a group message saying she was only in Geneva for one week, flying back to Malawi on 30 December to spend New Year with her volunteer team. She's an amazing woman.

Her new 'family' of vulnerable charges are lucky to have such a Mother Theresa. I wrote back, wishing her a Merry Christmas and a Happy New Year. Gael sent a thumbs-up emoji. No one else replied.

To know what is happening with Simone, you'd need to read certain kinds of gossip sites. Her second husband is on the board of one of Switzerland's biggest banks. Even if the events of two years ago had never happened, she would have dropped us eventually. Her social circle does not include ex-university mates/conspirators.

The only one I worry about is Gael. Journalists with good memories and emotional intelligence eventually figure things out for themselves. That's why I keep in touch, sending her silly memes about the current state of European politics and checking in at birthdays. If she has any questions about what happened on the first of January two years ago, I want her to come to me first. For her sake, I hope she never does.

Passwords should be memorable but not obvious. Meaningless to anyone but the five of us. Mine is 1999OddNumbers2019.

Chapter 29: Gael, Two Years Later

It's a strange sense of sadness when you lose a friend. Not through sudden death or terminal illness, just the knowledge they want you out of their lives. When Clark told me he would come to Brussels to visit, it was a cushion to soften the blow. He wanted out, permanently. That hurt, but I couldn't blame him.

My familiar connection to Lovisa and Simone fractured along with their friendship. Sisters in every way but blood, they were now distant acquaintances in fewer than twenty-four months. That hurt us all. Lovisa poured all her maternal feelings into her work and the beneficiaries of that huge heart are very lucky people. Simone's feelings, if they can be described as such, are entirely self-interested. After the pandemic was over, I travelled to Geneva over half a dozen times for my job, but never saw either of them. There was not a whiff of future reunions. Our entire closeness had been based on a fallacy. What was the point?

Mika and I remain in contact, albeit loosely. That makes sense. He wanted a thin line of cotton linking us, so that when I worked it out, I'd talk to him. He underestimates me. I worked it out long ago and went two steps further. If I was about to blow the whistle, the last person I'd go to would be Mika.

Simone and Lovisa thought I bought their story. Mika wasn't sure. Clark knew I didn't. He understood me better than most. That's why he left when he did. He sussed that if I hadn't clicked yet, it wouldn't take me long. The thing that still makes my throat contract is that he locked me in my bedroom while they did what they did and got rid of the evidence. He gave me a bottle of Bailey's and an alibi. He made sure I wasn't there.

I'll never be certain exactly how they did it. Frankly, I'd rather not speculate. It can't have been easy, with Clark's arm in a sling and Lovisa wearing a bandage, so I'm guessing Mika was the workhorse and the others acted as restraints. My research shows the camper van was returned to the hire car company on the first of January at 09.47. The CCTV shows a tall Caucasian male dropping the keys into a post box. A Volvo pulls up behind; the driver gets out and into the passenger seat. The tall man gets in and drives them both away. You can't see their faces clearly and the Volvo's number plate is conveniently obscured by snow. Unless you knew them, you'd never be able to identify either. The video quality was crap, but I recognised them both.

The body, to my knowledge, has never been found. Believe me; I still check every Swiss news site before I open my emails. I would know. No unidentified Asian male's corpse has turned up on a ski slope, in a crevasse, buried under a boulder or even sunk to the bottom of a lake. It will, one day. And then, perhaps, we'll have closure. Or not.

I know what they did. I don't know how but the one thing I do understand is why. Because I wanted to do the same thing.

As for pursuing this as a story, no chance. Not because it's not newsworthy, it's bloody gold dust. I just can't take the risk. How shitty would I be to expose my friends? How stupid to implicate myself? How far would my old mates go to keep their secret? I think I can answer that for myself.

So the narrative remains the same. A tragic accident in 1999. Two decades later, a bizarre night of confusion, bitterness and anger, which put an end to our reunions. Enough is enough. Time to move on.

Anyway, what do I know? I wasn't there.

Acknowledgements

Thank you Florian Bielmann, Jane Dixon Smith, Julia Gibbs and Chris Curran

Message from JJ Marsh

I hope you enjoyed *Odd Numbers*. If you're interested in my next psychological drama *Wolf Tones*, the first chapter is included at the end of this book.

I have also written The Beatrice Stubbs Series, European crime fiction:

BEHIND CLOSED DOORS
RAW MATERIAL
TREAD SOFTLY
COLD PRESSED
HUMAN RITES
BAD APPLES
SNOW ANGEL
HONEY TRAP
BLACK WIDOW
WHITE NIGHT

And a standalone novel:

AN EMPTY VESSEL

I have also written a short-story collection:

APPEARANCES GREETING A POINT OF VIEW

For more information, visit jjmarshauthor.com

For occasional updates, news, deals and a FREE exclusive prequel: *Black Dogs, Yellow Butterflies*, subscribe to my newsletter: jjmarshauthor.com

If you would recommend this book to a friend, please do so by writing a review. Your tip helps other readers discover their next favourite read. It can be short and only takes a minute.

Thank you.

Wolf Tones

By JJ Marsh

Chapter 1

The call came just before six. He was tempted not to answer as he was rehearsing the final movement of Bach's Suite No. 5 in C minor. But he put his instrument aside and picked up the telephone.

They had seen him perform. They were impressed. They extended an invitation to audition. He received the news with humility and expressed his astonishment, acknowledging the honour. He said he was surprised. Shocked, in fact. That was what they expected to hear, of course. They warned him not to get his hopes up. It was an audition, nothing more.

Rolf assured them he understood. He would take this in his stride. In truth that was an understatement. He could barely breathe as excitement and escape routes from his current situation thundered through his mind like freight trains, whistling their potential.

He pulled his attention back to the handset. He remembered to say thank you when they wished him luck and ended the call. He paced the tiny apartment, seeing nothing but the carnival in his head. In three weeks his life could change forever. *Our lives*, he corrected himself. Should he call her and tell her the news immediately? Or wait till she got home? He would calm down, cook a celebratory meal and tell her over a glass of wine. He couldn't wait to see her face; glowing in the knowledge her faith in him was validated. He grabbed his jacket and ran down four flights of stairs, so light on his feet he seemed to be flying. The stench of boiled cabbage and mould didn't touch him because his mind was already sampling coffee and pastries at a riverside café.

At the supermarket, he grabbed a packet of pork chops at 20% off and a bottle of Hungarian red. Whether it was any good, he had no idea. That was yet another area where Leonor's expertise exceeded his. *But if I get the job* ... he corrected himself again, thinking positively. *When I get the job, we'll drink wine every day!* He broke into a jog on the return journey, for no other reason than an excess of energy.

The sparse and cramped apartment, which usually depressed him when he opened the front door, failed to bring him down today. He stood at the threshold, mentally transforming it into their new quarters. Instead of one room doing double duty as his study by day and living room in the evening, he would have a music room of his own with French windows opening onto a lawn. Strains of Mendelssohn would float across the grass as wild birds added their natural accompaniment. Their kitchen would be the size of this whole apartment, an island in the centre where Leonor would experiment with fresh ingredients she had bought at full price. They'd have a wine rack and expensive cookware and Turkish rugs and a group of young, talented friends round for dinner.

He put the wine and the cheap chops on the small kitchen table under the window which served as their dining room and found an out-of-date packet of instant mashed potato in the cupboard. Even his limited culinary skills were up to chopping an onion and making a sauce for the meat. She would come home to a feast, at least by their standards. He put some Bartok on the stereo and hummed along as he cooked.

This was his moment to win; he just knew it in his gut. He was hungry for success. There was a time when he considered this apartment a step up, but now he could see it for what it was. A step up for him, a long fall down for her. Comparisons with her ancestral home were a waste of time, but he couldn't help thinking of those crenelated towers, the buttressed walls, the huge works of art, the grand piano, the stables, the sweeping gardens down to the lake. Now she was reduced to three parsimonious rooms they could barely afford on his orchestra pittance and her income as a music teacher.

Her sense of humour had kept them going. She would make him laugh by describing the apartment in real estate agent terms. Bag a Bargain in Bratislava! A bijou residence in an up-and-coming suburb, with a view of three countries and even if you can't quite see the Danube, you can smell the brewery. He'd join in, describing the rooms as if finding some joy in their failings. From the roof of their block you could see three countries, that much was true. To the north-east, the rest of Slovakia. That blue haze to the south was the border with Hungary and a mere twenty-minute journey to the west lay Austria, land of *Schnitzel*, confectionery and Mozart.

Austria! Things were about to change. This was a new reality. He'd been invited to audition. That kind of opportunity comes once in a lifetime and he would not let it get away. A sharp pain made him wince. Blood seeped from a cut on his index finger, contrasting with the white chopping board and the thinly sliced onion. Her voice rang in his ears, as clearly as if she were in the room. *Look out for your hands, Rolf! Treat them gently. They are your instruments.* He wrapped a tissue around his finger and focused on what he was doing. Making her a meal was an act of love. Her idea of an act of love involved more energy, bare skin and sometimes a little seasoning, but fewer ingredients. Just him and her.

He ignored the pulse in his groin and opened the window before he started frying the onions. Leonor hated coming home to the smell of cooking. She said she smelt it all day at school and home should be a rest from a constant assault on her senses. Delicate aromas of pear or sweet peas, subtle tastes such as smoked salmon and most importantly for her ears, silence. He checked his watch and switched off the string quartet. She was due any time in the next twenty minutes.

Because it was a Friday evening, she should be in a better mood than usual. She would enjoy the meal, rejoice at his news and sitting at the kitchen table, plan the audition strategy. She'd know what pieces to choose, how best to show off his skills. If it weren't for her, he'd still be a mediocre violinist.

Leonor had always watched him closely. She was the first to notice his upper body strength and long thing fingers would be better suited to the cello. *It has a depth, a melancholy. Just like you. You just need to spread your legs a little wider.* His groin twitched again as he recalled her mouth splitting into a wicked smile.

Leonor was the one who found him the best teacher. An ageing virtuoso who had long since refused new apprentices, he made an exception for her. 'Your father was a great friend to me. We can come to an arrangement,' he told her, with that simian smile. Rolf recalled those long afternoons with Jakobisku with little fondness, if he were honest. The man's revolting face snapping out criticism and contempt, exacerbated by the scent of mothballs and body odour made each lesson last an eternity. Yet the younger man's talent had flourished under his tutelage and although it was impossible to deny his mentor's influence, Rolf was coming into his own. He shook himself. Time to focus on mashed potato.

The door slammed shut just as he was uncorking the wine. His nerves fluttered, listening for any sounds to indicate her mood. Keys left in the lock, not flung at the wall. Coat and shoes off inside the door, bag rested on the floor, not dropped from a height. All good signs. He poured two glasses and waited for her to appear.

Leonor von Rosenheim stood at the entrance to the kitchen, leaning against the door jamb, her expression quizzical. "What's all this?"

He'd been rehearsing what to say from the moment he put down the phone, but now he just drank her in. Her lean, muscular form, her strong jaw and that incredible pair of dark brows arching over her hooded eyes. Even when she came home to him every night, even though she had an insatiable need for his body, he still couldn't believe his luck. Leonor von Rosenheim, who could have had anyone she wanted, chose him.

"Whatever's in that pan is burning," she said, flicking her gaze to the stove. He flipped the chops, turned down the gas and handed her a glass of wine.

"I had a call today," he said, remembering his lines.

Her voice dropped as her pupils dilated. "A call? Tell me more."

"I'll tell you everything. Sit. We're having pork chops with mash and onion gravy. And a glass of Bull's Blood."

Their eyes locked as they drank, a smile teasing the edges of her mouth. He folded up two pieces of kitchen towel as napkins, splattered a dollop of mash on each plate, added a chop and poured over the gravy. He closed the window so the draught would not ruin the ambience and sat opposite her, failing to suppress his grin.

She thanked him for the meal and sliced into the chop. "This is exactly what I needed. The food, the wine and the good news. Come on, then. You got a call. Don't tease me," she said, looking under her eyelashes.

He swallowed and tried not to get overexcited. "The board of an orchestra telephoned. They asked me to an audition. This is my chance, Leonor. This is what we've been waiting for."

She placed her cutlery on the table and clasped her hands to her cheeks, her eyes lit up by the light over the stove. "An audition? So soon? That is the best news! *Na zdravie*, my love! I am so happy for you! Here's to the Windy City!"

His glass kissed hers and they drank, holding each other's gaze.

"Can you believe it? I'll have to rehearse like crazy and choose pieces to demonstrate what I can do, but we can work on that together."

She scooped up some potato and gravy, her expression intense. "Yes, we need to choose carefully, look at their suggestions and repertoire. Then we rehearse as if our lives depend on it. How long do we have?"

He picked up his chop to gnaw the meat from the bone. "Three weeks. They're paying my fare and hotel, so we don't need to worry about finances."

She stopped chewing and took a swallow of wine. "Three weeks? Are they crazy? We won't even be able to get visas in that time!"

"Visas? Why would I need a visa for Austria? They're paying first class train travel from here to Salzburg. I will have a compartment to myself and can keep my cello by my side the whole time. In Salzburg, I have a hotel for two nights, one before the audition and one after. I suppose the second night is in case I get a recall."

Seconds ticked past as she stared at her plate, saying nothing. He replayed his response, questioning himself. Was he being insensitive? He had only stated the truth.

She resumed eating, flashing him a bright smile. "This pork chop is delicious. Did you make the sauce yourself?"

"It's not as good as one of yours, I know, but for a kitchen amateur, I was pleased. You know, we could probably afford another ticket if you wanted to come too."

"We could. If I used up the money for the gas bill and bought no groceries for three weeks, we could stretch to a second-class seat for me to accompany you. While you recline in your compartment with your own private butler. Maybe I'll just stay here and defrost the fridge."

They ate in silence until their plates were empty. He racked his brains to think of a way to recover the ambience but failed.

She spoke first. "If you pass the audition, then what?"

"*When* I pass the audition," he gave her a hesitant grin, still wary of her temper. "Then I'll start on the bottom rung. But even at that level, we'll have a bigger, nicer apartment, because the orchestra have accommodation for its members. You can still teach because Salzburg is filled with music students and I'll work like crazy to become a first cellist. We can go up in the world! I mean, back up in the world in your case. It's what we've always wanted, no?" He waited for her to lift her gaze from her plate, hoping for the best.

When she did, a smile spread across her face. She pressed her glass to her lips but instead of drinking, dipped her tongue into the red wine, lapping like a cat. "You are what I've always wanted. Shall we have an early night?"

He was out of his chair before she'd put down the glass. Her libido was always intense at this time of the month and he took full advantage, no matter how exhausted it left him the following day. Their lovemaking was ferocious and her desire unquenched even after the bells rang midnight.

Her breathing grew heavier and he stared at the ceiling, spent. If this hint of success increased his sex appeal to such a degree, God help him if he actually landed the role of cellist with the Salzburg City Orchestra. Salzburg. He knew nothing about it, other than the Mozart connection. No idea as to its location to other Austrian cities, its geography or climate. Her words echoed in his head.

'An audition? So soon? That is the best news! *Na zdravie*, my love! I am so happy for you! Here's to the Windy City!'

He stretched an arm out to locate his phone on the bedside table, cautious and slow. If she woke for another bout, he wouldn't have the energy. She slept on. He deepened his own breaths, faking a light snore and typed 'The Windy City' into a search engine. The results pointed to Chicago.

Chicago? Was that why she mentioned visas? Why on earth would she assume his audition would be in Chicago? He replaced the phone and closed his eyes. Some days, he had no idea how her mind worked.

Printed in Germany
by Amazon Distribution
GmbH, Leipzig

19277619R00129